THE MOON TOUCHED CHRONICLES

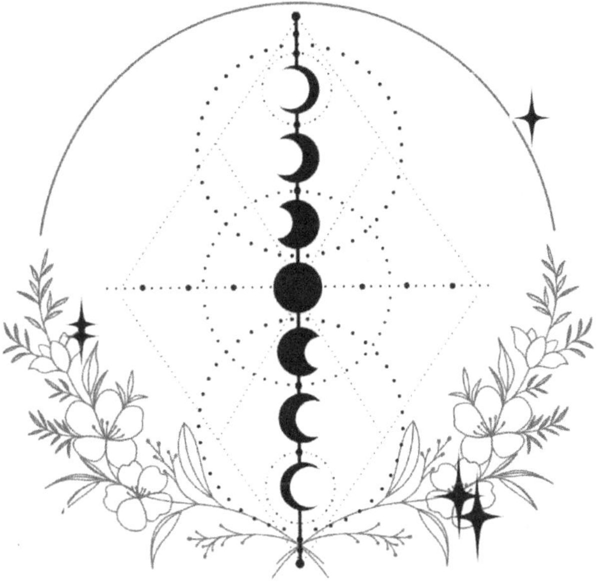

Nightfang

RUBY ELLIS

For the one who holds the other half of my soul.

Thank you for making every day an adventure.

Content Warning

This book contains strong language, sexually explicit scenes, primal play, discussions of drink tampering, violence, kidnapping, trafficking, child neglect, societal infertility, pregnancy, childbirth, and loss.

While this book does contain darker topics, the romance in this book is not dark.

Table of Contents

Prologue

"21 baby!" Ramsey's voice fills our tiny apartment as she crashes through the door. She is just coming off of a long shift at the hospital. Several nurses have called in sick this last week due to a nasty virus that has been going around. Luckily, Ramsey has been able to avoid catching it. She is a stickler about handwashing and has been putting on a mask before she even enters the hospital, but I have been taking extra shifts at the coffee shop just in case she needs to call in sick. All of her paid sick days have come and gone already this year.

"Are you sure you feel okay going out tonight? I understand if you are too tired. We can celebrate some other time." I can see the exhaustion in her eyes before she masks it with her 'I'm totally fine' look.

"Absolutely not. We are going out to celebrate your 21st birthday in style. It is already planned. I was able to snag a table at the new club on 46th. Reese has her fake ID now and I know the bartender who is working tonight so she will only need it to get past the bouncer."

"If you're sure…"

"I am sure. Don't argue with me on this. I never got to do the whole clubbing thing when I turned 21—we are going to do this right. For both of us."

I squeal as I excitedly hop around our apartment.

"Reese should be home from class any minute. I am just going to grab a quick shower and then we can head out for some dinner. Carbs will be our friend tonight!"

"You are the best, Rams." I give her a hug and then head into our shared closet to start pulling outfit options for all three of us.

"Happy Birthday, Ro!" Reese pulls me into a hug as soon as she gets home, dropping her school bag on the floor by our feet. "Is that what you are wearing?" Her cheeks tinge pink as she looks at the dress options, I have pulled out for us.

"This is actually what I had picked out for you." I hold the dress up to her body, pressing the fabric tight to her curves.

"What? I can't wear that!" Reese gasps and pushes the hanger away.

"It is just a dress, Reese." I can't help but laugh as her eyes dart nervously around the room. "Also, I'm kidding. This is definitely *my* dress for tonight. I thought you might want to wear this one." I hold up a more modest version of the tiny black dress I plan to wear.

At 19, Reese is far more innocent than Ramsey and I are, but you wouldn't know that based on the smutty books she reads.

We all work together to do our hair and makeup. My blond curls are slicked back into a sleek ponytail. Ramsey has her hair half up, making her brown hair flow down her back like a chocolate fountain. Reese's red hair is impossible to tame tonight, so we embrace the crazy and let her fiery curls do their thing.

"Remember that you cannot take your medicine tonight if you drink any alcohol," Ramsey reminds Reese as we leave our apartment.

"Yes, Mom." Reese replies cheekily.

The night air is cool, but we do not wear jackets. None of us want to have to keep track of anything other than each other tonight. We swing by my favorite pizza place on our way to the club, grabbing our much needed carbs for the night. We normally wouldn't take a taxi, but since it is a special occasion, Ramsey insists that we can afford it for tonight.

Money is tight. We honestly shouldn't be going out at all, but it is something that we have talked about for years. We were not always lucky enough to be able to spend birthdays together, so now that we can, we go big.

"Are you sure that I can get in?" Reese looks worried, though there is excitement in her eyes too.

"The ID looks legit. Once we are through the door, you won't even need it anymore," I assure her as we wait in line to get into the club.

"What if we get caught?" she whispers, looking around anxiously.

"We won't."

"But what if we do?"

"Then we will deal with it," Ramsey says, putting her arm around Reese. "But Ro is right. We just need to get you through the door. You won't be ordering your own drinks. We are mostly going to dance. A few of the young doctors were talking about this club. The DJ is supposed to be amazing."

Reese nods her head as a smile tugs at her lips. Out of the three of us, Reese is not one to break the rules. She is the total opposite of me in many ways.

Even when we were all kids, Ramsey was more of a parent than a sister. Reese is the young, innocent rule follower. And I, well, I am the wild card. Impulsive. Most likely to cause problems. I can feel the need to create chaos swirling in my belly as we wait in line to get into the club.

The hotties definitely showed up to play tonight. I catch the eye of a guy standing with a group of his friends a few feet ahead. I offer him a smile, which he returns with a panty melting smile of his own.

Tonight, I am here with my sisters—so I will not be hooking up with anyone. But I might need to put in the effort to start dating again. It has been months since my boyfriend and I broke up and getting myself off in the one-bedroom apartment that I share with my sisters is really not an option for me.

While we wait in line to get inside, I pull out my phone and sign back into my Tinder account. There has to be at least a few men in New York who are interested in swiping right.

Safely inside the club, we all let out a breath of relief. Getting Reese in with us was the trickiest part of the night. The chaos of the pounding base, flashing lights, and people on people is like a balm to my soul. I always feel better when the outside world matches the frenzied energy in my brain. Ramsey heads straight to the bar, pushing through the crowd of people waiting for their drinks until she comes face to face with a very handsome bartender. When he sees her, he pauses making the drink in his hand to flirt with her. Clearly, this is the guy who was able to get us the VIP booth that we are now being led to.

Ramsey pulls out her phone, selecting the Notes app where she has listed out all of the drinks we plan to order. A few nights ago, we looked up a list of the dirtiest named drinks we could find and used that to make our selections. Cum shots, obviously. Pink Panty Droppers. Sex on the Beach. Frisky Kitties. Muff Diver. Screaming Orgasm—I think we could all benefit from one of those. You get the idea. Reese was not home when we made the list and the look on her face when Ramsey starts listing them off is quite possibly going to be the best part of the night.

We do not want to get too drunk—so we only order one of each so that we can try them all without dying from alcohol poisoning.

We drink, we giggle, we dance.

Then the world goes black and everything that I thought I knew is changed forever.

Chapter One

Keep running. Exhaustion eats at me. My body has long been pushed past its limit, but I need to keep moving.

Stay alert. I can barely hear the sounds of the forest over the blood rushing in my ears and my heavy breaths filling the air. Birds chirp. Twigs crack. My bare feet pound into the forest floor, bruised and bloody, as they lead me away. Bringing me to safety—I hope.

I need to find help.

I need to keep running.

Two days ago, I awoke from a nightmare. My body was sluggish, but my mind was suddenly alert. The drugs had slowly leached from my system but I don't know where I was. The world around me is vastly different from the towering buildings that have always been the backdrop to my life. Now, trees surround me. Plants and roots and rocks. Each breath fills my burning lungs with air so fresh, it is like I am learning to breathe for the first time in my life. So different from the hell that I just escaped. I am never going back.

I will run until I find help.

I will die if they catch me.

Memories of the past trickle in, like I'm slowly waking from a dream—not fully awake but not asleep either.

I was at the club with my sisters. It was my birthday. 21. We drank ridiculous drinks and danced to amazing music. I could feel the booze enter my system. But it just made me feel loose and free. Until it didn't.

My sisters and I planned to stay together. But we got separated in the mass of bodies gyrating on the dance floor.

The hot guy who smiled at me in line found me on the dance floor. He wrapped his arms around my middle, pulling me tightly to him so that he could grind his boner into my ass.

The drinks are making me feel out of control in a way that I am not used to. I don't like it. So, I politely turned down my dance partner and headed back to our table. I was sure that my sisters would meet me there, but I never made it. The flashing lights in the club and the loud music disoriented me further. I stumbled into people, confused and dizzy.

I noticed the bar up ahead instead. I thought that if I made it there, the bartenders could help me find my sisters. But once I was close enough to make eye contact with my sister's friend, he gave me a slow, creepy smile.

That is the last thing I remember before the world around me blurred and faded into blackness.

Then a cage. My time spent in the cage is jumbled, fuzzy, confused.

Cold.

Alone.

A sharp pinch.

Darkness.

I woke up and ran.

Are they hunting me? Did I escape? Or is this a trap, a game?

What would Ramsey do? She is the responsible one. She would know what to do right now. She would...assess the situation. Make note of any damage.

Hunger eats at my belly as exhaustion burns my limbs. My throat scratches as I swallow, desperately clinging to any moisture it can find.

My face aches and the world blurs around me. One of my eyes is mostly shut—swollen. Bruises paint my body. Purples, blues, yellows.

I was beaten.

Flashes of pain and hot rancid breath. Cigarettes and booze. Sneering eyes that stalked me. Trapped me. Caged me like prey.

Was I... Did they... Assess the situation. Make note of any damage.

I am only wearing my bra and panties. I reach a shaky hand down to check myself. No blood. I'm not sore to the touch. Good. That's good.

I refuse to go back, so I run. I need to find help. Are Ramsey and Reese okay? I need to find my sisters.

I am getting closer to something—I don't know what—but I can feel it. I have been running almost nonstop for two days towards this pull that I feel.

I hear a buzz in the air—like there is too much static, or maybe a lightning strike. The air is sucked out of my lungs and the pain that follows feels as though my organs are being shifted. I am being remade in this static void.

Unable to withstand the pain, I fall to the ground and curl up onto my side, ready to die. It was stupid to think that I would come out of this alive. My entire life has been leading to this point—passed from one home to another, half-starved and nearly forgotten. My sisters are the only bright stars. Ramsey kept us alive and brought us back together as soon as she could. Reese, so young and resilient, always made the best out of whatever life threw at us. I hope they are safe. I hope they are looking up at the same moon, knowing that I am too. One last time. Turning my head at the sound of a branch snapping, I come face to face with a wolf.

This must be a dream. A gentle way for my brain to ease me into the nothingness of death.

The wolf is huge. Admittedly, I have never seen a wolf this close before—but this one must be at least double the size of a typical wolf. All black. Ice blue eyes that pierce straight to my soul. Beautiful. Majestic. One hundred percent a figment of my imagination. Real wolves cannot look like this. Flecks of navy swirling in a puddle of silver. These are eyes that cannot happen in real life.

I reach out and the wolf moves closer, slowly. Is it here to reap my soul? Will it ferry me over the river? Maybe it is just waiting for me to die so that it can eat me.

I snort. That would be my luck. Kidnapped, drugged, caged, then eaten by a wolf. At least he is pretty. I guess there are worse ways to go.

I'm so tired, I hardly feel the pain anymore. I just stare at my imaginary wolf until darkness takes me again.

Chapter Two

Heat envelops me as the fires from Hell burn my body. Sweat slides off my skin. If I am honest, I didn't think that I would actually end up in Hell. Surely a few tickets and helping to sneak my sister into a nightclub isn't enough for eternal damnation. Maybe my soul was already marked. A previous life damning me to tragedy after tragedy. It would explain all of the shit I had to deal with as a child.

My body aches all over but I do not actually feel burned. It is more the ache of exhaustion. Like I was overconfident at the gym and now I am paying for it. Groaning, I try to sit up. To look around. But I cannot open my eyes. They are glued shut with overtiredness—like I haven't slept for days.

Despite being in Hell, it feels as if I am resting on a cloud. Soft cushions surround my body. Tranquil. Comfortable. Quiet. I always thought that there would be more shrieking. Demons flying around, causing chaos. I definitely envisioned the creepy ass flying monkeys from Wizard of Oz to be in Hell. So, maybe I am somewhere else.

Maybe it was all just a strange dream, and I am dealing with my first ever hangover.

Hushed voices fill the air as I drift in and out.

"She cannot learn if you take her patient away," a quiet woman's voice says.

"She can learn with others. Not here," a more demanding man replies.

"It was just a mistake. And you caught the error before it caused any permanent damage," the woman says.

"That is not good enough," the male voice growls.

"Okay," the woman concedes before sleep pulls me back under.

When I wake again, the room is silent. The voices that I heard before are no longer present. Forcing my eyes open, I see only my imaginary wolf staring back at me.

Sitting up abruptly, I gasp, realizing that I am in a bed of furs and blankets, naked, snuggled up next to a wolf—who feels very real, if I'm being honest. His inky fur is soft and smooth. He is lying so still, I might not believe he was alive if not for the rising and falling of his chest and gentle whimpers.

I guess it wasn't all a dream. Where am I? I look around the room and see that I am in some sort of yurt. I must be outside of the city at some sort of camp or commune.

"Hello. That's a good boy," I reach out my hand for the wolf to sniff. I have no idea what in the actual fuck is happening right now, but if the wolf didn't eat me while I was dying on the forest floor, or while I lay naked and vulnerable in bed, maybe it is a friendly wolf.

The wolf cocks his head to the side but then nuzzles his face against my hand.

"Okay. That's a good start. My name is Rowan. Do you have a name? Or maybe a human who can answer since I just realized that I am talking to a wolf as if it would be able to answer me," I ramble. "Thank you for not eating me," I add for good measure.

I try to get out of bed, but I start to feel dizzy. The wolf lunges towards me, forcing me to lay back down.

"You're right, Big Guy. Maybe I should keep resting for a bit."

I look around the room some more. It is pretty big. The bed that I am in has to be at least a king size. A freestanding bathtub resides on one side of the room while a stone fire pit dominates the center. An orange glow from the hot coals fills the room with heat and a low light.

One of the foster families that I lived with for a while was big into health retreats. Is that what this is? Hopefully they have some real food. I am so hungry, I don't think that a fancy juice is going to cut it.

I look around for some clothes. I can hear movement outside the tent—maybe there is someone out there who can help me. I need to find a way home to my sisters.

"Hey Big Guy," I say to the wolf. "Do you think you can point me in the direction of some clothes? Or food?"

The wolf stares back at me as if he doesn't understand what I am saying. Fair, I guess. I sit up again, letting the blankets pool around my waist. Maybe there is a shirt or something laying around.

Suddenly, the door flaps open and an elderly woman walks in. She is tall and strong. Maybe they are onto something with all that wellness and hippie shit. I scramble to cover my naked body, suddenly self-conscious of my scrawny arms and visible ribs.

"Oh good, you're awake." Her voice is calming despite the command in her tone. I believe that this is the same woman I heard before. "It was a little touch and go there for a while. We were not sure if you would make it." She comes over to my side and begins poking and prodding at my bruises. She puts her hand on my forehead, "And your fever has broken. Good. Get up. Let's get you clean."

"I'm sorry. Who are you?" I asked hesitantly.

"My name is Heka. I am here to heal you," she says.

Okay. Well, she is definitely more of a holistic healer than a doctor, but I am not complaining. I really do feel better. And she can probably help me get back to my sisters.

"Can you tell me where I am? How did I get here? Is this your wolf?" I gesture wildly with my hand towards my new snuggle buddy.

Heka chuckles and shakes her head. "Warrick will answer your questions. But first, let's get you cleaned up. You have been asleep for seven days. I brought some food with me. You can eat while they fill the tub."

"While who fills the tub?" As soon as the question is out of my mouth, the door opens again and in walks two very large men carrying buckets of steaming water. I gasp and make sure that my body is covered. The wolf jumps up onto the bed to cover me as well. Is he protecting me?

The wolf lets out a low growl causing the men to hurry with their task. Heka chuckles.

This has to be one of the weirdest experiences of my life. Top five, for sure.

Once the tub is filled, Heka helps me stand. When it appears that she is not going to give me any privacy, I shrug my shoulders and drop the blanket that I had wrapped around myself. Besides Heka, the only other set of eyes in this tent belong to the wolf. I doubt he will think anything of my nakedness.

The bathwater stings as I lower myself into it, but the hot water does feel nice on my achy muscles. Heka grabs what I am assuming is some kind of soap and begins washing my body, being mindful of my bruises. I haven't seen a mirror, so I do not know the full extent of my injuries, but my face feels less swollen and the bruises that I can see are starting to fade.

When I am cleaned, Heka helps me dry off with a fur and then wraps me up in another one. I sit close to the fire while I eat some of the food that Heka brought with her.

I thought about not eating it, just in case it is poisoned, but I am so hungry. I doubt she would have taken the time to help work the snarls out of my hair if she wanted me dead. Right?

"Do you have any clothes?" I ask. Heka is wearing a flowy Mumu style dress. She is taller and broader than me, but I would take anything over feeling this vulnerable.

"Here is a shirt that you can put on. I will try to find you something closer to your size after I leave. But Warrick will want to talk to you as soon as you are done eating."

"Thank you." I lower the fur that I was wrapped in and slip on the shirt. It is massive—dropping all the way down to my knees. But it is comfortable in a well-worn kind of way. I'm assuming it belongs to Warrick—whoever that is. This is probably his tent.

I finish eating the berries, dried meat, cheese, and bread that Heka brought for me. It all tastes good, but I was so hungry, I probably would have eaten my left foot.

When Heka leaves the tent, the wolf follows her outside. Huh. I was kind of hoping that he would stay to guard me while I wait for Warrick. I didn't realize it before but the wolf's presence made me feel safe. Now that he is gone, I start to panic.

I can't stop the tears that leak from my eyes. I try to control my breathing. In-2-3, Out-2-3. Three things that I can feel—the soft fabric of the shirt, my wet hair, the heat from the fire on my skin. Three things I can hear—the crackle of the fire, voices outside—

The door opens again and in steps the largest man I have ever seen. He must be pushing 6'8". He is solid muscle. The thick cords of his arms are covered in black tattoos. His chest is bare, showing a very defined v leading down to his...

Oh my holy mother fucking god. He is wearing leather pants, but they are not properly fastened, as if he got dressed in a hurry, and they do nothing to hide his massive erection. He is huge. Everywhere.

Who is this guy?

I know that I have never seen this man before in my life, but there is something so familiar about him. Though I probably should, I don't feel like I am in danger. This is the kind of man people feared. Clearly powerful. Hopefully he will want to help me find my way back to my sisters.

Realizing that I am completely eye-fucking the hell out of him, I clear my throat and offer up an introduction.

"Hi. You must be Warrick? Heka told me that you would answer my questions."

"Hello, Rowan. You can call me War. I am pleased to see you are well. Did you get enough to eat?" I am still hungry, but I do not want to seem ungrateful for the kindness that was shown.

"I did, thank you. Um, can you tell me where I am? I don't remember getting here. The last thing I remember is seeing the wolf and then nothing."

"My wolf found you and we brought you here to keep you safe and to heal. You were beaten and bloody. Heka believes that you developed an infection, which is why your fever was so high."

"He is your wolf? Will he be coming back in here?"

"I'm sure you will see him again soon." He smirks. "Do you remember anything else? When you arrived, you were almost naked, only wearing scraps of cloth. Your feet were scraped from the forest floor, and you had bruises covering your body."

Unsure how much to say, I decide that it won't do me any favors leaving out the limited details that I do know. If I want to get back to my sisters, I am going to need help. I weirdly trust his wolf, so I am hoping that I can trust him too.

"My memories are a little bit fuzzy. But, I was separated from my sisters while we were out dancing for my birthday. I think that I was drugged and put into a cage. I don't know how long...but I ran from them when the drugs were wearing off. They got sloppy and did not lock the cage. I don't know what forest I escaped into, but I felt something guiding me through the woods. I don't know how to describe it. I just had a feeling that it was where I could find safety. Then, there was an electrical zap, pain, your wolf, and then nothing. I woke up here."

War's jaw ticks and his hands are squeezed into fists at his side. Is he mad at me?

"I promise nobody will hurt you like that again."

He is mad *for* me. I let out the breath that I didn't know I was holding.

"Is this some kind of wellness retreat or a commune situation? I don't mean to offend you, and I am truly grateful for the kindness that you have shown me, but I need to get back home. How far are we from New York? I don't have any money on me, but if you can help me home my sisters will reimburse you. Ramsey is a nurse. We can find her at work if she isn't at our apartment when we get there. Both of my sisters will be so worried."

I don't think that this is a hostage situation, but I read once that if you make yourself seem even more human by telling your captor about your life and loved ones, you are less likely to be murdered.

Warrick is huge, but I can tell that he is trying to make me comfortable. He isn't standing over me, but is crouched in front of me. His face, while naturally strong and sharp, is softened with the way that he is speaking to me.

"I'm sorry. I don't know where that is. There are a few permanent villages in my territory but most of the land is undisturbed, fit best for the way that we move throughout the area following the wild herds. Right now, we are a small group of about 30. Mostly men, though some families choose to stay with us as well. And of course, Heka."

Trying to process what is going on, I ask, "You haven't heard of New York City? The Big Apple? Home Alone Lost in New York? Annie?"

"I do not know what most of that means."

"Okay." My breaths become sharp. "Excuse me for one moment." I cover my head with a blanket and start crying as panic grips me once more. What does he mean he doesn't know what that means? Even if I was in another country, he would have heard of New York City, right?

After a few moments, I feel the wet nose of the wolf poking under my blanket. I let him in, wrapping my arms around his neck and crying into his fur. By the time I am able to get myself under control, I lift the blanket to see that War has left.

It is just me and the wolf.

"I guess it's just you and me, Big Guy. I'm sorry I got your fur wet. You are a good boy. I just don't understand what is happening right now."

No closer to going home than I was before, I snuggle with the wolf and fall fast asleep.

Chapter Three

When I wake up next, the wolf is gone, and War is asleep in a chair by the fire. There is no way that he is comfortable. Getting up, I walk over to him and place my hand on his cheek. His eyes open, alert.

"Are you ok? What's wrong?" He scans my body and then the room, looking for any threats.

"I'm ok. Well, physically, I'm fine. I am really confused as to where I am. But I wanted you to know that you can sleep in the bed. I can take the chair. You barely fit here."

His face softens. "I'm ok in the chair. My wolf will not allow you to sleep anywhere other than my bed."

His wolf will not allow it? I guess I wouldn't want to go up against that toothy fur ball either.

"Well…" I look around the room as I try to find another solution. "Then I will share it with you. The bed is plenty big enough for both of us. Really, all three of us can fit when your wolf comes back."

I don't know why I suggest it. The idea of sharing a bed with a complete stranger is probably one of the craziest things I have done. But this is clearly his home. He chuckles and shakes his head but lets me help him out of the chair. We crawl back into bed, leaving at least a foot of space between us.

"Goodnight, War."

"Sleep well, Rowan."

War

There is no way that I will be able to sleep while laying in bed with Rowan. While she was healing, I slept on the floor next to the bed. I could not leave her while she was so vulnerable, especially after I found Heka's apprentice administering the wrong medication. Once she woke, I tried to sleep in an extra lodging, but my wolf would not allow it. I do not understand how she got here to our land, our time, but it is obviously different from her own.

The world that I live in—this world—is diverse. There are many species of beings that all call The Mother home. Because there are so many different species throughout our land, our bodies have evolved into being able to understand and speak in all languages. Even though we live in different territories, it is still necessary to be able to communicate with each other for travel, trade, and resolving disputes. So, while I technically understand every word that she is saying, most of it does not actually exist here. I first heard her language while she spoke during her fever. It was mostly nonsense, but it was enough to trigger my language adaptation. We were unsure when she would wake up, so Heka and I made an effort to speak in her language while we were in the room with her. Just in case.

But she doesn't realize that we speak different languages.

She doesn't even realize that my wolf is as much a part of me as I am him. Anyone from this world would assume that we are one and the same. But not her. Her assumption that we are separate just adds to the mystery of where she is from.

I did not mean to mislead her. At first, I did not want to scare her by having her wake up to an unfamiliar face. I wasn't sure if she would remember my wolf, but I knew that he would be more calming than seeing a strange man who is so much larger than her petite frame. Then, I didn't want to scare her by shifting in front of her.

She has already been through too much. Drugged? Beaten? Caged? What horrors lived in her world that would do such a thing to her?

Shifters are common enough throughout the territory, but she was talking about cities that don't exist, and I had a feeling that seeing a shift happen would be shocking to her already confused state.

Now, I do not know how to tell her because I do not want her to think that I lied. I can't lie to her. My wolf would not allow me to be dishonest with his Mate...our Mate.

Rowan is our Mate. Our perfect match. The one who holds the missing piece to our soul.

Wolf shifters can only find their Mate through their wolves. Sure, it is possible to pair up with non-Mates to appease a sexual appetite, but a True pairing is that of Mates. Claimed by the wolves that exist with us.

My wolf claimed Rowan before she even appeared. She talked about following a pull while running away from the fucking bastards that had her caged. Well, we felt the same thing. My wolf was out hunting for the pack when we both felt the tug. The need to find whatever it was leading us toward.

I split from the group immediately—no longer interested in tracking our prey. Once we caught the trail of our Mate, there was no other option but to find her.

We came upon a small clearing in the forest and stopped. Waited. Suddenly, Rowan appeared in front of us, battered and bloody. Completely exhausted and holding on by a thread. She looked in our eyes and my wolf knew that she was ours.

She is our True Mate.

Once separated by time and space, apparently, now brought together. In the blink of an eye, she appeared out of thin air.

I have never heard of a wolf finding a Mate in another species. I do not sense a wolf within her—and if there was one, surely she would have shifted to both heal and protect herself. Shifting can speed healing and would make her bruises disappear completely. No, she must not be a wolf. But then what is she? Who is she? How did she get here?

Her breathing is even as she sleeps peacefully next to me. I fight the urge to pull her into my arms. During her recovery, I slept on the ground next to the bed, needing to be close but not wanting her to be uncomfortable waking up next to a stranger. Her body took much longer to heal than what we are used to. She is fragile.

In two weeks, I will claim her under the full moon. Now that my wolf has found her, we cannot be apart for longer than a few days. It would drive us to insanity. Claiming her under the moon will bond us together forever. It would link her body with mine, giving us both the strongest features of the other.

She may get a wolf. Or, at the very least, she will receive my lengthened lifespan and accelerated healing. There are some non-shifters throughout the territory, but they all only live for a maximum of 100 years. Wolf shifters can live to be over 1000 years old.

Other than a True Mate never being previously found in a non-shifter, wolves rarely choose a non-shifter as a lover because they are just so fragile. Breakable. Prey.

We need to seal the bond so that she is safer, stronger. Protected by my name, my wolf, and my pack. Hopefully I will be able to convince her.

I am one of the strongest Alphas in all of the territories. My brothers rule over the other territories.

Separate packs, separate territories, united through blood.

After the full moon, we will travel to our family home in the center of our territories. I will ask my brothers to help me find Rowan's sisters. If they were brought here like she was, hopefully they will know how. My brother Griffin has an extensive library. Maybe an answer can be found there.

Tomorrow, I will explain my world to Rowan.

Chapter Four

Rowan

When I wake up the next morning, I am alone. I reach over to feel the bed where War slept last night. It is still warm. He must have just gotten up a little while ago. The fire is burning in the ring, keeping the chill of the morning at bay.

Stretching, I wrap a blanket around myself and make my way closer to the fire. Sitting in the chair that War was trying to sleep in last night, I chuckle. I am 5'5" and the chair fits me perfectly. I do not know how he physically got his massive body folded into it. Truthfully, I am not sure why he even owns it.

What in the world am I going to do? I think that I am well enough to travel. If I could just find a bus station or a car service, maybe War will give me some money to pay for it. There has to be someone here who knows how to get back to the city.

My stomach rumbles as the door to our tent opens. War enters with a tray of food and two steaming cups of what I hope is coffee. Working as a barista, I have become somewhat of a coffee snob, but I will gladly take any form of caffeine right now. Preferably by the gallon. And in an IV. I must have been in really rough shape if I slept for over a week and still feel this level of exhaustion.

"Good morning," I greet, offering a friendly smile.

"Good morning," he replies. "Did you sleep well?"

"I did, actually. I only woke up because I had to pee and was hungry. It looks like you were already a step ahead of me. Is there a bathroom around here that I can use?" I can't help the blush that colors my cheeks, feeling slightly embarrassed that I need to talk about normal bodily functions with this gorgeous god of a man.

Am I ovulating right now or does he look even better early in the morning?

He grunts in affirmation and then sets the tray down on the table next to me before taking my hand and walking me out of the back of the yurt. Apparently, this is my bathroom. Lovely.

"I will give you some privacy," he says as he walks a few feet away, turning so that his back is to me. I look around. I can hear others moving about but we seem somewhat secluded.

"Can you, um, cover your ears or something?" War snorts but raises his hands over his ears. I pee as quickly as I can, refusing to ask about toilet paper, and thanking whatever gods are watching over me that I did not need to do more than relieve my bladder.

Following War back into the tent, he leads me to my seat by the fire, draping a warm blanket over my legs before nudging the food closer.

"Thank you."

We both eat off of the tray, though he is giving most of it to me. It is probably his way of letting me know that it is safe to eat. Not that I thought it wouldn't be. I feel incredibly safe with both War and his wolf, despite the circumstances.

When the food is mostly gone, he stands and starts pacing—as if he is nervous.

"What's wrong, War?"

"Nothing. Everything is fine. I, uh, want to show you around our camp this morning so that you can get some fresh air. You were sleeping for a week, and you must be itching to get out."

"That sounds wonderful, actually, though I'm not sure I am dressed appropriately to be out in public." I tug at my hair, a strange combination of stringy and frizzy from sleeping with it wet. The shirt that I borrowed is comfortable, but I am not wearing anything underneath it. Though it is massive, it is still pretty revealing.

"You look fine," he tells me. "Our hunting party is aware that you have been recovering. Some of the females have been the ones to help Heka while my wolf stood guard. I am sure that they would like to see you up and moving around."

I hadn't even considered that others might have already seen me. After waking up yesterday, I have felt pretty isolated despite knowing that there was an entire camp outside these walls. "Oh. Okay."

"But, before I show you around, there are some things that you need to know about us. About my people and our world."

"Okay... I live in New York. I'm sure there isn't anything that you can say that would really shock me. Trust me when I say that I have seen it all."

"What I am about to tell you, show you, is probably not anything you have heard or seen before. Because I do not think that you are from this world. I do not know how you came to be here, but the places that you speak of, well, they do not exist here. The language you are speaking, while I can understand it due to the evolution of my species, is not a language that has ever been spoken here before. The clothes that you arrived in, are not made of the same materials that we have here."

"But, how? That isn't possible. How can I be in a different world?"

"I do not know, Sunshine, but there is more." His eyes soften towards me, though he still looks nervous to tell me more.

"More than me being in a different world? How am I going to find my sisters? What if they are here too? They could be alone and scared."

War kneels down in front of me, taking my hands in his. "I promise you that we will find your sisters if they followed you into this world. My brothers and I will work together to search all three territories. But there is more."

"Okay," I say. Putting on a brave face when really, I'm not sure if I can process more.

"We are shifters—me, my people, my brothers. Our wolves live inside of us, and we live inside of them. My wolf is me."

"What? Like a werewolf?"

He thinks for a minute before responding. "A werewolf isn't a thing that I know here. But we can shift between man and wolf whenever we want. Right now, I am Warrick the male. But Warrick the wolf is still aware inside of me. He can hear through my ears and see through my eyes. He can hear my thoughts, and I can hear his—though he has more instincts and feelings versus words."

I stand up and begin pacing. "So, every time you are here, your wolf is too—even though I can't see him. And when he is here, you are too—even though I can't see you?"

"Yes."

"And everyone here is a wolf shifter? Men, women, children? Heka? Oh, god... you saw me naked." My entire body flushes at the thought. "You were here when I took a bath. Heka didn't tell you my name, I told you—or your wolf at least."

"Yes...to everything. Everyone in our pack is a wolf shifter. In our world, there are other kinds of shifters and also some non-shifter species. The majority do shift though. We are born with our wolves, so even young children are able to shift into pups. Heka is my grandmother, though we live such long lives, we don't usually refer to each other as such. And, I did see you naked. I apologize for that, but my wolf would not let you be alone without one of us present. It is for your safety. And nudity is common here anyway. Shifting can tear through clothes, so we usually strip before shifting to save from needing to constantly repair things. There are many who go without clothing altogether."

He is telling me all of this as if this is a normal conversation. Somehow, while running away from what I am assuming were drug or sex traffickers, I ended up being transported to another world where wolf people live. I'm about 80% sure that this is all just a bad trip from the drugs that were being pumped through my system. But then I remember the pull—and the zap—followed by a pain so intense it felt like I was being split apart and remade.

"The pull," I whisper as the feeling comes back to me. I can still feel it now.

"The pull is something that my wolf and I feel too. It is what led us to you in the forest that day."

"What does the pull mean? Is that a shifter thing? It feels quieter now." As if being here has settled it a bit. I rub at my chest.

Taking my hands in his again, he guides me back over to the chair. Sitting down, he kneels in front of me. "There is a legend that talks of our first peoples. We used to be wolves, unable to shift. Trapped in our true forms, we were happy amongst our packs, but it felt like half of our souls were missing. The First Alpha asked The Mother for help. He wanted to find the rest of his soul. When The Mother blessed The First Alpha with his second form, he was able to shift and found a piece of his missing soul. But it was still incomplete. He went back to the Mother and asked again for help. The Mother blessed him with a True Mate—the keeper of that missing piece. Because the wolf keeps the largest portion of our soul, only the wolf is able to find our True Mate."

"True Mate. Like a soulmate? I traveled to a different world and time and found my soulmate?"

"Yes. That pull we feel is our souls calling out to each other."

"Like magnets."

He smiles. "It is calmer now because we are together. If we are separated, it will feel stronger."

"So, if I find a way back home, what would happen?"

"If we are separated, the pull on our souls would eventually cause madness."

If I go home, I will go nuts? Is that what he just said? "I'm going to need a minute to process all of this."

"Take as much time as you need. There is more to discuss, but it can wait. Would you like fresh water brought in for a bath?"

I just nod, unable to produce words as my brain implodes. I am in a different world. My soulmate is a wolf shifter. If I find a way back home, I will most likely go insane. Because there is nothing insane about this scenario. Nope. Totally normal, everyday, kind of thing.

Warrick said that he would help me find my sisters—if they are even here. At this point, I'm not sure if I want them to be in this world with me or if I want them to be back in New York, safe, and with indoor plumbing.

I am pulled from my thoughts when I see the tub being filled up. The men must have left the water at the door, because War is the one carrying the water over. After he is done, he puts something in the water. It kind of looked like bath salts. I snort, realizing that even wolf shifters probably like a nice, relaxing bath now and then.

Not having moved from my spot, War gently grabs my hands and leads me to the tub. He pulls my borrowed shirt over my head and helps me into the water, making a point to look away—giving me privacy even though he has technically already seen my body.

War turns to leave the tent but I stop him. "War, can you please stay?"

He looks shocked by my request but quickly agrees. "Of course."

"I just feel better when either you or your wolf is here, though I guess that is really the same thing, huh?" My tone has a bit of bite to it. I can't help but feel a little upset.

"For what it is worth, it was never my intention to mislead you. I just did not want to scare you."

"I know. It is just a lot. I might need you to be patient with me as I make any of this make sense in my head."

"I'm not going anywhere. Go ahead and relax. I will be here when you are ready."

I don't know how much time passes while I am in the tub. At one point, the water starts to cool, and War dumps another bucket of hot water in to warm it back up.

I still don't know what any of this means. And I have plenty of questions. But I do feel safe with War. For some reason, I believe him. What he explained about my clothes and my language not being of this world. What he said about the pull and his explanation of True Mates. War has felt familiar to me from the very beginning. Maybe it *is* because my soul recognized him. I never really believed in soulmates before, but this does feel like *something*. Something new. Something old. Something right—in a way that defies logic. And his eyes, they are the same as his wolf's. But I need to see it. Using a fur to dry myself off, I step out of the tub and turn to face War.

"Strip," I command.

He raises his eyebrow.

"I want to see you shift. I don't know if I will fully believe it is even possible without seeing it first."

The corner of his lip ticks up into a half smile, settling into a smug smirk. Keeping eye contact with me, he slowly undoes the fasteners on his pants. He is already shirtless. Maybe the one that I was wearing before is the only one he has. He pulls at the leather strings, loosening up his fly before dropping his pants to the floor.

Holy fuckballs. His cock is enormous and hard. He doesn't take his eyes off of me as he reaches down and gives himself a few hard tugs, probably trying to relieve some pressure. I'm not even sure if he knows he is doing it. Watching him sends a bolt of electricity straight to my clit. I press my thighs closer together, trying to relieve some of the aching in my core. It is then that I realize that I am, yet again, without clothes.

"Are you ready?" he asks as I openly eye fuck him.

"Mhmm." It almost comes out as a moan. I need to get a grip.

He chuckles and then within seconds, War's body transforms from the beautiful, naked man into the wolf. Huge body. Black fur. Same blue eyes that War has. I didn't notice the similarities before because I wasn't looking for them. Who in their rightful mind assumes that the wolf that rescued them could also be a man? I crouch down to my knees, still only wrapped in fur, while the wolf walks over to me. I let him nuzzle his face into my neck—scenting me, I realize.

"Thank you for finding me," I tell him as I wrap my arms around his neck in a hug. "I was running from a pretty scary situation and seeing you brought me comfort—even if I thought I was hallucinating and dying at the time."

Looking around for some clothes to put on, the wolf nudges open a chest. I pull out a fresh shirt.

"So, you do own more than one. Is the naked chest thing just for my benefit, then?"

The wolf chuffs. I smile when I realize he probably just laughed at my joke.

Chapter Five

Dressed only in a shirt, War and I step out into fresh air. The forest surrounds us on three sides; War's yurt is backed up against a large rock formation. The trees that surround us are huge—some as big as the giant sequoias that I have only seen pictures of. They reach so high, it looks like their top branches can touch the clouds that decorate the bluest sky I have ever seen. Smaller trees and bushes also fill the ground, leaving only small paths for us to walk on. There are several smaller yurts sprinkled between openings in the trees. There are both people and wolves walking throughout the area. Everyone smiles or waves when they see us, though nobody approaches.

War leads me over to a tent that is about half the size of his. We enter the space without knocking—something that will take some getting used to.

Sitting by the fire in the middle of the tent, is Heka.

"It is good to see you up and moving around. How are you feeling today?"

"Much better, thank you." I sit down next to her. After I am settled, War makes his exit, briefly mentioning needing to discuss some issues within the pack. After he leaves, Heka and I sit in comfortable silence while she makes me some tea and I gather my thoughts.

"War filled me in on a few things. I was hoping that you might be able to answer some more of my questions."

"I can definitely try." Heka says as she hands me a steaming cup of liquid.

"War told me that you are his grandmother. I truly mean no offense when I say that I am hoping that your age might help me find some answers."

Heka chuckles. "No offense taken. I am very old— nearing 900."

"Holy fucking cannoli," I say, the words leaving my mouth before I can stop them. I can't believe I just swore in front of a 900-year-old wolf shifter grandma. "Oh my god, I am so sorry. It is just that nobody from my world lives that long.”

Heka cackles at my blurted words, making me feel a little less bad.

“Have you ever heard of someone coming over from a different world?”

“Not that, specifically. Though there are many, many species within our world. We all had to come from somewhere. It is possible that not everyone originated here. As wolves, we believe that this is where we have always been, but who could really say how the first firsts came to be?”

“War said that there are non-shifters here as well. Are they human, like me?”

“The term ‘human’ has never been used as far as I know, but it is possible that some are. There are a few different species of non-shifters. There are some that I have seen that look similar to you, with slight variations in features. Others are vastly different with scales or antlers—as if they are permanently partially shifted.”

“Huh. I am just having such a hard time making sense of all of this. It is so different from everything that I have known to be true. Did War tell you that we are maybe, possibly, probably True Mates?”

"You either are, or you are not. His wolf would not be wrong."

"Is that a common thing? To find your True Mate?"

Heka pauses, collecting her thoughts before she answers. "Not anymore. Many years ago, our population was concentrated, not spread out so much throughout the land. It was more common to find a True Mate then. Over time, it became less and less. True Mate pairs have a higher success rate with reproduction—most likely due to True Mates being genetically perfect for each other. Because our life spans are so long, it is possible for one member of the pair to be late in life while the other is just being born. With less Mates being found, and less babies being born, True Mates have become a rarity."

"But I don't have a wolf. How can I even be an option?"

"That, I do not know." She wipes her hands, picking up a basket of herbs and adding them into a bowl to mash. "But War's wolf found you and in doing so, found his true pair. Just because it has not happened before, does not make it any less true."

It feels like I am living in a fairy tale—or one of the romance books that my sisters enjoy reading. I make an effort to stop thinking—to stop trying to force what is happening around me into a mold of what I am used to. If

I focus on feelings alone, I have to admit that there is truth to it all. I was pulled, literally, to another world. I was aware, on some level, that it was happening, and therefore it was real. The connection between War and I hums inside my chest. It is so present that it shocks me that others cannot hear it buzzing. Focusing on the pull, I can tell that War is still close by. If I looked outside, I would probably find him within eyesight of the door. But how can I find my way back home if we can never truly part?

"What does this all mean? For me? For War? How do we navigate this?" I ask out loud.

"That is something that the two of you need to discuss. But, now that you have found each other, you cannot be apart. You will find a way. Together."

Finishing up the tea that Heka had shared with me, I stand to leave. "Thank you, Heka."

"Of course, child. I'm always here to help if you ever need it."

Walking out of Heka's home, I see War across the way, but I do not go straight to him. I need to work some things out in my head before we continue our conversation. I make a lap around the village. This place looks like an outpost—somewhere for travelers to stop if they need to rest but it clearly does not house a large group permanently. I can feel War's eyes on me, tracking my movements as he talks to members of his pack.

One of the men he is talking to looks to be in charge. Not in a higher rank than War, but maybe his second in command. I cannot hear what they are saying, but I know that he needs to make sure that the pack is still running now that he is not so focused on my recovery.

There are two other men and one woman who are contributing to the discussion. Despite War's efforts to move away from her, the woman keeps reaching out and touching his arm. It is not overtly sexual, but she is definitely acting like she is *very* familiar with him—or wants to be. Flaming hot jealousy burns in my chest, despite only just having met War.

Before I even understand what I am doing, I march over to where they stand, positioning myself between them. Even though I am much smaller, I use my body to force the woman to step back. Then take War's hand in mine to lead him away from Miss Grabby Hands.

"Is everything okay?" He asks once we are a few feet away from the group, a smile tugging at his lips.

"Yep. Peachy. I was just hoping that you might introduce me to some of the pack." I cannot believe that I just did that, but I pat myself on the back for not admitting to him how jealous I was—even if he might have suspected it.

"Of course. Zeke!" The man who I pegged as his second walks over to join us. "Rowan, this is my Beta, Zeke. He is my second in command. If you ever need something and cannot find me, he will be there to help."

Zeke stands tall. Not quite as tall as War, but he still towers over my human sized frame. Unlike War, his hair is cut short. And his expression is kept controlled. It is hard to tell what he is thinking. If we were back in my world, I would assume that he served time in the military.

"It is nice to meet you," I say, holding out my hand for him to shake. He clasps my arm—not quite the handshake I am used to—before grunting in acknowledgment. Not a chatty guy. Got it.

War quickly finishes his discussion with Zeke before leading me around the village. We see mostly men, in both human and wolf form, but there are also some women walking with pups. I smile, tickled by the fact that those pups are their children.

There are only a few kids, but they run from their parents to play around us, some jumping on War's back as he wrestles them to the ground.

As War plays with the children, some of the women approach me. All of the women are at least 6 feet tall and have more muscles that I could ever dream of building. Most of the women offer warm greetings and are happy to see me up and moving around. They all seem curious about me, but do not pry—which I am grateful for. I don't even know what I would tell them.

One of the mothers introduces herself as Eden. She is a mother to two of the pups. She told me that her True Mate is one of the hunters in War's pack. And, when I am ready, she will happily answer any questions that I might have.

By the time the sun starts to set, I have met all but one of the women in the pack—the woman who was getting handsy with War. I tried approaching her, but she turned away, not allowing me the chance to introduce myself.

Returning to our tent, my stomach rumbles and my eyes feel heavy.

"Dinner will arrive shortly," he says. War puts more logs on the fire, bringing it back to life. It is chilly again this evening. Since I only have one of War's shirts, I grab a blanket and sit closer to the flames.

"What would you be doing if I wasn't here?"

If he is surprised by my question, he doesn't show it. "Typically, I would be out hunting for the pack. That is what I was doing when I found you. Most of the men in our pack are hunters. They leave during the day to find prey and then return with their kills, sending another group out once they have returned. There are some women who hunt as well, but most of the women help process the meat so that we can bring it with us when we move on. You met most of the women and families that are traveling with us today."

"How often do you move?"

"It depends on the movement of our food source and the weather. My wolf is able to communicate with the other wolves in our pack, mind to mind. We called all of our hunters back this afternoon to set up a new hunt before we depart from this outpost. Most of us will move out in a few days. Some will stay behind. One of the women you met today will stay here with her pup and her Mate. They live here permanently."

"Eden?" I try not to sound disappointed. I was hoping that she would be traveling with us.

"No, Eden and her Mate Arlo will be coming with us. Arlo is one of our strongest hunters. Their pups will be traveling with us too."

"Do families always travel with a hunting party?"

"No. That is up to the pair. But because Eden and Arlo are True Mates, they cannot be apart for long. I offered them permanent stays in the big village or any of the outposts, but they enjoy traveling. They only stay in the large village when Eden is swollen with a child.”

The food arrives and we eat without saying much of anything. Dinner tonight is a delicious stew. I dunk the crusty bread into the broth and let out an embarrassing moan when the flavor hits my tongue. War makes sure that I have had my fill before eating the remaining food that was sent for me.

“If you need to leave to help hunt, I understand. I don’t want you to give up your responsibilities to hang out with me.”

War shakes his head. “You are my top priority. We will stay here until you fully recover. Then we will move on, working our way towards my family home.”

“Then...well, maybe you can bring me on a hunt with you? I have never done that before—but I would like to learn.”

He looks unsure for a moment before his eyes begin to soften. “Okay. But you will need to stay by my side and follow my instructions. There are dangers in this world that you are not accustomed to.”

“I promise.” I offer him my pinky as a promise but quickly lower my hand back down to my lap when I realize that my wolf man does not know what I am doing.

"And we will stay close to the outpost," he continues. "You are not well enough for a long journey."

I nod my agreement. Much clearer than holding my pinky in the air between us.

Crawling into bed, I shiver. The fire warmed the room, but the furs on the bed are still cool to the touch. War slides in next to me.

"I can sleep in my wolf form, if it would make you more comfortable."

"That's ok. I'm not uncomfortable around you. I'm just a little cold."

War closes the gap between us, pulling me flush against his hard body. "Is this okay?"

I melt into his heat. "It's perfect," I purr.

We lay there silently for a while. I think he might have fallen asleep, but I cannot turn my brain off.

"War?"

"Yes, Sunshine?" My heart flutters at the endearment.

Turning in his arms so that I am facing him, I ask the question that has been on my mind all day. "What does all of this mean for us?"

War remains silent for a long while. Most likely as unsure as I am as to how we figure this all out.

"It means that I am yours, and you are mine. Fully. Completely. In any way that you will let me." His words are so sure that I have to believe they are the truth.

I have never had someone to call mine—not really. I gulp down some air, trying to steady myself. Looking up, I study his face. He seems sincere in everything that he tells me. It is finally starting to sink in that this isn't some super complicated prank or a cult that is set on brainwashing me. I am not going to end up in an A&E documentary. I really am in a different world.

I saw him shift. He turned from man to wolf and back to man right in front of me. I saw kids who shifted between human and pup while playing.

Looking closer, I cannot deny my attraction to War. He is the most beautiful man that I have ever seen. Even more than the physical attraction, I feel completely safe in his arms. A part of me feels like I have always known him. Like he has always been a part of me that I had just not discovered yet. And, maybe it is some twisted Stockholm syndrome thing—but I think that it really is my soul calling out to him.

"So, do we date? Is marriage a thing here? Are wolves monogamous? I have seen quite a few nature documentaries and animals seem pretty loosey-goosey when it comes to mating."

War lets out a low growl. "We do not share."

"Okay, Big Guy, that is good." I place my hand on his chest. "I am definitely a one wolf kind of girl."

Placated by my answer, his growl stops. "Are you ready to continue our discussion from this morning? There is more that I want to tell you—need to tell you—but I do not want to overwhelm you."

Pulling away from his body a little, I settle on my side so that I can see his face while we talk. "I can handle more."

War looks into my eyes before nodding. "There is a ceremony that we will have under the next full moon. Being True Mates, our souls are already pulling us together—connecting us. By marking you under the moon, our bodies will also be connected. Typically, when True Mate wolves bond, the strongest attributes of both are shared. Someone who is a Beta, for example, will rise in power to match their Alpha."

"But I'm not a wolf. I don't have any powers. There isn't any magic at all where I am from."

"To my knowledge, a bonding has never been done before between a wolf and a non-shifter. There have been relationships between different species, but the ceremony and sharing of powers can only be done between True Mates. It may awaken latent powers within you. Or, it could just transfer some of mine over to you. Most importantly, it will help to keep you safe. You will heal faster, live longer."

I can't believe that I am seriously considering doing this—but I have always been a bit impulsive. And do I really have a choice? How am I supposed to survive in a world where literally everyone is stronger than me? And our soul sharing thing means that I can't be separated from War anyways. Either I stay here and make the most of it, or I try to find a way back home and bring War with me. Would he be able to survive in a world where he could never really be himself? I couldn't ask that of him or his wolf. But this sounds like marriage with magic. Am I ready for something like that? Either way, I need more information.

"What happens during the ceremony?"

"It has two parts. First, is the public claiming under the moon. Surrounded by the pack."

"And the second part?"

"A more private claiming to seal our bodies together as one."

"Sex?"

War nods. "It is a little more than that though." He takes a deep breath before he continues. "When wolves bond, the pair are forced into a specialized heat which can last days."

"Days?"

Nodding, he continues. "If your anatomy allows, I would give you my knot."

Recalling a dragon shifter romance book that Reese convinced me to read a few years ago, my eyes go wide. I glance down, trying to picture what that would even look like.

"You have a knot in addition to that giant trouser snake you are packing?" War barks out a laugh. Whispering to myself, I say "I'm going to be split in half."

"I would never hurt you." Leaning in closer, he brings his lips to my ear. "You were made to be my perfect match. I will stretch you slowly and make sure that you are ready to take all of me into your tight cunt."

A cross between a whimper and a moan escapes from my mouth, warmth spreads throughout my body. "And...um...that would happen for days?" How am I going to survive this?

"For the claiming, yes. Though I would very much enjoy it if it continued to happen after that as well." Then he winks at me. Winks! This huge, wild, wolf man winked at me.

The pressure in my core is almost unbearable. I know that he can smell my arousal—I can feel it slicking my thighs. But he does not attempt to act on it, keeping his hands in a respectful place. I bet he knows how to fuck. He seems like he is into some rougher, kinkier things—and to be honest, I really want to find out.

I have fooled around with a few guys, but I have only had sex with one and he wasn't really into trying new things. Basic vanilla sex was a major reason why I broke up with him. I have used toys on myself and experimented a little, but there is only so much that you can do by yourself.

War has probably had plenty of experience figuring out what he likes. A twinge of jealousy aches in my chest as I think about that woman with her hands on him. Realistically, I know that he must have been with others. He is over 100 years old already. But I do not like the thought of him with anyone else.

Seemingly unaware of the spiral my mind is spinning, War lifts his hand to my cheek. "We should get some sleep, Sunshine."

Nodding, I roll to face away from him. War pulls my back flush to his front and puts his massive hand on my belly—holding me in place.

Yawning, I say a quiet, "Good night, War."

As I close my eyes and start to drift off to sleep, I feel the press of his lips to my neck and hear a whispered, "Sleep well, love."

Chapter Six

War

On the morning of the hunt, Rowan is still sleeping, tucked into my side when I wake. She looks so perfect. Her blond hair is wild across the pillows. Her cheeks are flushed from sharing my body heat. The shirt that she is wearing has ridden up and I can feel the swell of her bare ass against my body.

My cock is so hard it feels like it is going to bust out of my pants. I usually sleep naked, but Rowan has let me hold her tight to my body each night and I do not want to push for more when she is not quite ready. She chooses to wear clothing while we share a bed, so I follow her lead.

Sliding out of bed, I make sure Rowan is tucked in, not letting any of the cool morning air give her a chill. I stoke the fire, not adding more logs since we are leaving this morning to go on the hunt. After several days of additional rest, and Heka's assurance that Rowan is healthy enough to leave the camp, I have arranged for us to join the hunting party that is departing this morning. There is a herd of vakusa grazing in a meadow not far from here. Because of their size, vakusa take several hunters to fell an adult, but they are typically docile creatures.

The herd is not far, so Rowan and I will walk to the meadow while the other hunters in the party will surround the herd and push them towards us.

But first, I need to find her some breakfast. Gathering what I need from the camp's stores, I head back to wake my sleeping Mate. Gently brushing my fingers over her temple, I speak softly. "Sunshine, it is time to wake."

She jolts but then sinks further into the furs. "Five more minutes," she grumbles. I chuckle. She is definitely not a morning person.

"We need to head out if you want to join the hunt this morning."

"Is the sun even in the sky yet?"

I laugh again. "Almost." I bring the food closer, hoping that it might help entice her out of the blankets. "Are you hungry?"

She takes a peek, groaning when she sees that I brought her some of the cobbler that we enjoyed last night for dessert. "You don't fight fair." Sitting up, she keeps her lower half tucked under the blankets while she reaches for the treat.

As soon as the sweetened fruit hits her tongue, she moans—a sound that makes my already hard cock twitch. "That good, huh?"

"It really is. I'm not even embarrassed to admit it."

Walking towards the meadow, Rowan is often distracted by the beauty of our world. It is not yet the warm season, though plants are beginning to make their appearance again. The hardier, brightly colored leaves that decorate the forest floor sway as we carefully walk through them. There are some established, maintained trails that lead from outpost to outpost throughout the territories, but the paths that we take while hunting are organic. We do our best not to disturb The Mother.

Rowan lets out a surprised gasp as a pod of tremblies scurry out in front of us. "What are those?" The small four-legged animals scamper up into a nearby tree.

I smile. "Tremblies. They usually make their homes in trees like those." I point out the large, reddish-brown trees. "In the warmer months, the leaves on those trees turn a bluish purple, like the fur of the tremblies."

"They are beautiful. We have squirrels and chipmunks in my world but we don't have anything colored like that where I am from."

We continue on, stopping every time that she sees something interesting. The hunting party is ready for us, but I tell them to wait until we arrive to start the hunt. I can feel irritation from a few of the hunters, but Arlo openly laughed through the bond. He has been bonded to his True Mate, Eden for decades, but he remembers what it was like in the beginning. There is very little that I would ever deny Rowan.

Creeping slowly as we approach the meadow, I reach out to hold Rowan's hand. She steps right up beside me, looking out at the herd of vakusa in front of us. I look around, making sure that this is an okay place to position Rowan while the hunt begins. "These look just like capybaras but massive. I can't believe that this is my life right now."

I smile, happy that she is finding joy in being in this world. "You should be safe here. I am going to shift and join the hunters—unless you would like me to stay here with you."

"I'll be fine, Big Guy."

"If you need anything, just say my name. I will be able to hear you."

"Go. I'll be fine, I promise."

She sits down on a large rock, positioning herself so that she can see the entire meadow.

Stripping out of my clothes, I throw them to Rowan with a wink and then shift into my wolf, stealthily joining the hunting party as we work together to single out the vakusa that will be our prey. If possible, we always choose the most mature beast. One that is no longer bearing pups.

Vakusa are much larger than wolves, rising to the height of about 15 feet while standing on all fours. Wolves, on the other hand, are typically around 4 feet tall from foot to back. My brothers and I rise about a foot higher than most. That is why vakusa are typically hunted by groups.

Working with my pack, we are quickly able to separate one vakusa from the rest. Doing our best to not start a riot, we push our prey away from the group. While the beasts are docile, they will still put up a fight when pressed. The beast runs at us head on, kicking its legs out whenever we get close. Before any of us get close enough for the kill, a scream fills the air.

Abandoning the hunt, I race towards Rowan as a younger adult vakusa charges at her, huffing and roaring. The ground shakes under the force of the animal's heavy body as it tears across the meadow towards my Mate. I pick up my pace, sprinting after the rogue beast in an effort to cut off its route before it tramples her.

Without taking her eyes off of the animal, Rowan tries to back away, reaching behind her for anything that might help her to safety. I let out a mean snarl, warning the vakusa of my presence, but the vakusa is not deterred.

Feeling Arlo only a few paces behind me, we barrel past the vakusa and position ourselves between the beast and Rowan, growling and snapping our teeth. The vakusa stops in its tracks but continues huffing.

"What is making her do this?" Rowan asks, placing a shaking hand on my back.

I look around and listen, trying to find a reason for this animal to go rogue. It is not long before I hear the answer. Less than twenty feet away, hidden behind logs and brush, a baby vakusa grazes.

Trusting Arlo to continue providing protection, I shift and stand next to Rowan. "There is a vakusa pup nearby," I tell her as I nod my head in the direction that the babe lies in. It must have moved closer to Rowan after I left to join the hunt. It is strange for it to be here alone. Vakusa typically leave their young together, watched over by one or two adults in the herd.

Rowan's breathing evens out as she takes my hand and slowly moves us away from the pup.

"Whoa. It's okay, mama," she says. "I would never harm your baby. We will leave. Just let us leave. Whoa, mama." Her voice is quiet and steady as she talks to the beast.

Once we are far enough away, the vakusa lets us go, turning its back and quickly retreating to its grazing pup.

"How did you know how to do that?" I ask, pulling her into my arms for a hug.

"One of the families that I was placed with growing up had a daughter who was really into horses. Sometimes I went with to the stable where she took lessons, even though I wasn't allowed to ride. Some of the stable hands would let me watch them work while I waited. One time, there was a foal that was stalled with its mother. I just wanted to get a little closer, maybe pet the baby horse, but the mare freaked out. A worker helped calm the horse enough so that I could sneak away."

She looks across the meadow where the rest of the hunting party has finished taking down the vakusa we were hunting. "I'm sorry you had to miss the rest of the hunt."

I tilt her chin so that she is looking at me. "You are my priority. Always."

"Well, that is one way to get my blood pumping," she says as she calms her breathing.

"I'm sorry, Sunshine. The pup must have wandered away from the herd."

"It's not your fault." She wraps her arms around my middle, resting her cheek against my chest as she hugs me again. "Thank you for showing me a bit more of this world. Near death experiences aside, it is really beautiful here."

I look out across the meadow, trying to see it all from her eyes. Even in these cooler months, everything is vibrant and full of life. Based on what she has told me about the city that she lived in, I am sure that it is a stark difference.

I look down at Rowan. Golden hair, a tangle of curls that shine in the sun. Her cheeks rosy from the crisp morning air and adrenalin. Her eyes sparkling with wonder. Deep in my bones, I know that there is nothing more beautiful in this world than her.

The next morning, I step outside to make sure that my pack is getting things sorted to leave. Like I told Rowan, Gabriel and his family will be staying behind. They will make sure all fires are properly taken care of and will clean and close up all of the lodgings, keeping them ready for the next time we pass through. Because Rowan needed time to heal, we stayed at this outpost much longer than we normally would. The meat and hide from the vakusa that we felled yesterday will go a long way in restocking supplies that were depleted during our stay.

We travel pretty light. As a pack, we typically travel in our wolf forms and only carry small pouches with a few necessities.

I have yet to explain this to Rowan, but she will be riding on my back as we travel today. My wolf is plenty big and strong enough to carry her tiny form. We will be running pretty hard so that we make it there before dark.

I make my way into Heka's tent to make sure she has all of her medicines packed up and ready.

"Good morning child," she greets as I kiss her cheek.

"Good morning, Heka. Do you need any help? We are planning to leave in about an hour."

"I am all set and ready to go. This is not my first time, you know."

"I know," I say, chuckling. "We will be continuing on home after the full moon. Are you happy to be going back? I'm sure the lodge has missed you. My brothers were pouting that I brought you with me this time."

"It will be good to be home. I'm not as young as I used to be. Oh, here." She hands me a pair of leather pants. "I made these for Rowan. She will be too sore if she is riding on your back with only your shirt on."

"Thank you. I did not even consider that."

"Her skin has not been roughed up from years of living like we do. She will probably be sore even with the pants, but they should help. Come and see me when you get her settled tonight. I have some balm that will help too."

"About that other issue..." I start.

"She needs to find a purpose. If it is not healing, then you need to help her find something else."

I nod my agreement and then excuse myself. Stopping to pick up some food and return to wake my Mate.

Walking into the tent, I see that she is already awake, warming herself by the fire. "Good morning, Sunshine. Did you sleep well?"

"Yes, thank you." I set the tray of food down by her chair. "How long before we need to leave?" she asks.

"After we eat and get dressed." I start packing a small sack with some shirts and soaps. The next outpost should have everything that we need already there, but it doesn't hurt to have some extra in case we need to stop along the way.

When she is finished eating, I eat the food that is leftover. Then, setting the tray outside our door, I retrieve the leather pants that Heka gave me. "These are for you."

"Pants? And here I was just getting used to having my pussy free all the time."

I sputter and cough on my own spit. Did she just refer to her cunt as a feline?

She smirks. "You ok over there Big Guy?"

"Yeah." I clear my throat. "Sometimes the things that you say must not translate properly. For the record, I favor the idea of you not wearing pants, Rowan. Heka just thought that it would make you more comfortable while riding me all day."

This time, it is Rowan that starts to choke.

Realizing what I said, I clarify, "You will be riding on my wolf's back while we travel today. We always travel as a pack in fur."

"Oh. Okay. Are you sure you will be able to carry me?"

A growl from my wolf erupts from my throat. "You are tiny, please do not insult our strength or ability to provide for you."

She laughs. "That's not what I meant. I, um, have never even ridden a horse before. The closest I ever got was on one of those carousel rides at the carnival. But there really wasn't any risk of me falling off. You probably do not even have those here, huh?"

"I promise that I will not let you fall. During longer trips, I can strap you to me so that you can sleep while I run, but for this one, we should arrive before nightfall."

"Okay. I trust you."

"Thank you. Now, the next village should have everything that we need. It is larger than this one. We can probably even find you some more clothes that fit you properly. Though, we will be able to get things made specifically for you once we reach the lodge."

I watch as she slides the tight leather up her creamy legs. The need to taste her gets stronger every day. The scent of her arousal fills the air every night as we lay down to sleep. It smelled so good last night, I almost came in my pants without even touching myself. Realizing that I am watching her, she starts to blush. As she fumbles with the fastening, I walk over and help her tighten and tie the laces.

With her body almost flush with mine, there is no way to hide my cock from her notice. Her eyes flick down to see where my hands are and then back up to my eyes.

"Thanks," she says breathlessly.

Backing away slowly, I undo the laces on my pants and remove them slowly. Rowan watches me the whole time, not shying away from openly looking at my cock. Her tongue peeks out to wet her bottom lip before she bites on it softly.

With one final look into her eyes, I shift, giving myself over to my wolf once again. Rowan picks up my pants and places them in the bag that I had packed. She tosses the strap over her shoulder and then looks at me.

"So, how do I do this? I probably should have asked before you went all canine," she giggles.

Lowering down to the ground, Rowan climbs up to straddle my back, squeezing my sides with her thighs. She lets out a squeal and grips onto my fur as I stand. I chuff out a laugh and then walk out of the tent with Rowan safely on my back.

The rest of my pack has shifted and are waiting for us in the center of the village. Some of the kids are shifted, riding on their parents backs. It is difficult for them to keep up as pups.

I give the order to move out and then turn to lead the pack to our next destination. We spread out a bit as we run, not wanting to crowd each other. Zeke runs along my side. He has been taking over many of my duties these last few days while I have been taking care of Rowan.

"Has there been any word from the other packs?" I ask, mind to mind.

"Not much. Bade let us know that a member in his pack had another failed pregnancy. The bleeding and grief that followed almost took the mother."

"Was it a True Mate pairing?"

"No."

"Make sure Heka is informed." I feel his agreement through our connection. *"Regarding the issue that I was trying to discuss with you earlier, before we were interrupted, she needs to be dealt with. "*

"We could send her into Nighthowl to assist your brother's outposts," he suggests.

"I would hate to pass her off to him, but we might need to, " I agree.

Zeke moves away from my side, probably in search of Heka. The issues that wolves are having with fertility is bothersome and I do not know a way to rectify it. Ideally, there would be a way for wolves to more easily find their Mates—but there is no way to make that happen. Many of them are simply not out there yet. Mine came from a completely different world, for fucks sake.

If there could be a way to help expecting mothers maintain their pregnancies, even if it is not with a True Mate, then that could help to bring new wolves into the world. Pups used to always be born in multiples. My brothers and I are triplets, born from True Mates. Pregnancies now result in only one pup—if it is successful at all.

Griff was going to look in his library to see if there is any record of this happening before—or any insight on how to help maintain pregnancies without a True Mate bond. Unfortunately, the Alphas that lived before my father took over were not the best at keeping detailed accounts of the world. Bade was going to reach out to other shifter species to see if this is a problem that they are having as well. Wolves are not the only shifters that believe in True Mates. There may be an answer outside of our territories.

Lost in my thoughts, we run for half the day before Rowan gets my attention.

"Hey Big Guy," she reaches down to rub my neck, "is there any way we can stop this train for a potty break?"

I swear I have no idea what she is actually saying half of the time. This time, I understood enough, though. I put out the call for everyone to take a short rest. Finding a semi-private spot in the woods, I lay down so that Rowan can slide off of my back. When she does, I shift back so that I can communicate with her more easily.

"Does that request mean that you need to relieve yourself?" I confirm.

"Of course. What else could a potty break mean?" She looks around to see that we are alone and then makes a spinning motion with her finger. I turn around and make an effort to not roll my eyes. Apparently seeing each other naked and snuggling together every night does not mean that she is comfortable enough to urinate in front of me yet. She still makes me cover my ears too—which is laughable all on its own because it does absolutely nothing to stop me from hearing.

Chuckling, I explain, "A pot is used for storing, though I doubt you want to put your urine in a container."

"Ew... Okay, I'm all done." I turn back around to see her in the process of pulling her pants back up while she walks closer to me. She trips and I catch her, pulling her body into mine.

"Well, hello there," she says while looking down—most likely talking to my erect cock.

I wink, seeing no point in trying to hide my desire for her. I help her re-tie her pants and then grab my pants out of the pack strapped around her. Usually, I would not bother. My pack has seen me naked countless times before. But, again, it seems like something Rowan feels is private, and I want to make her comfortable.

Me putting on pants does not prepare her for the sight of my entire pack, either still in wolf form or shifted and completely naked, sitting around eating lunch.

"Holy biscuits and gravy, that is a lot of hairy balls. Is that even sanitary?" Her words fly out of her mouth in a loud whisper.

Realizing that I do not like the idea of her seeing other males nude, I cover her eyes and lead her back away from the pack and sit her down on a fallen tree trunk.

"I will go and get lunch. You wait here," I say.

Rowan just stares straight ahead with pink cheeks. Laughing at her reaction, I quickly gather some food and return to her side.

"Are you doing ok over there?" I ask.

"I promise I'm not a prude—I'm just not used to so many giblets hanging free. Nudity isn't allowed in public where I am from."

"It just comes with being a shifter. It will become normal for you too."

Rowan slides over and I sit on the log next to her. We talk while we eat our lunch. She tells me a little bit about her sisters and the city that she grew up in. I share some stories about my brothers and the trouble that we caused our parents while growing up. It is really nice. Comfortable.

After about a half hour, I shift back into my wolf form and we run the rest of the way to our destination.

As the sky begins to darken, we arrive. I carry Rowan right into my tent without stopping to introduce her to anyone. There will be time for that later. She has been quiet for the last couple of hours, and I think that she might be in pain. She started shifting as if she was uncomfortable, trying to keep her inner thighs from touching my back.

Once in the tent, I shift without warning, immediately reaching around to hold her in my arms and keep her from falling. She winces when I scoop my arms under her legs. Carefully carrying her to the bed, I ask her if she is okay but looking at her tear-filled eyes, I already know the answer.

Chapter Seven

My thighs are rubbed raw. I don't need to look to know how bad it is. What started as a mild irritation has turned into what feels like blood running down my thighs. I probably should have admitted that I was in pain, but I didn't want the whole pack to have to stop just for me.

I would look over and see kids happily riding on the backs of their parents, unbothered by the constant rubbing. I figured that if they could tough it out while wearing nearly nothing, I could handle some discomfort.

About an hour or so ago, it went from bad to worse. I have spent the last portion of our journey blinking back tears and holding in sobs, embarrassed that something as simple as riding has proven to be too difficult for me.

War carries me gently to the bed. He asks if I am okay but then must see in my face how not okay I really am.

"I am so sorry, love." It comes out as a low growl. "Why did you not tell me?"

"I th...th..thought that i...it would be ok. I d...d...didn't want to slow the p..pack down." My words come out shaky in between sobs.

"I would have shifted and walked the rest of the way with you in my arms. Please do not hide your pain from me."

"I'm sorry."

He steps to the door of the tent, giving someone an order before returning to my side.

"Heka is going to bring something for the pain. But first, we need to get you out of these pants and see what is going on. Would you feel more comfortable having Heka help you?"

Taking a deep breath, I try to prepare myself for the pain. "No, you can help me. Please just be gentle. It feels like my skin is shredded."

War nods and then undoes the ties to my pants. Very gently, he lowers the waist over my hips and past the curve of my ass. Then, he hesitates. He inhales and I know that he can smell my blood and whatever else is oozing out of my thighs.

"It's ok. I can handle it."

I gasp as he very slowly pulls the leather away from my battered skin—first one leg, then the other. Once they are past my thighs, he pulls my pants off the rest of the way and drops them to the floor.

"Is it ok if I look closer?" he asks.

I nod, knowing that while he is going to be up close and personal with my lady bits—there is nothing sexual about this. He needs to make sure that it is all surface level wounds and not something more serious.

As he is looking me over, the door flaps open. War growls and covers me with his body.

"It is just me, child. No need to show your teeth," Heka says. "Rowan, I have medicine for the pain and a salve that will help protect your skin as it heals." Pushing War off of me, she looks at my wounds and then turns to War. "You can help heal this as well," she tells him.

War nods and then covers me with a fur from the bed. He growls again while two men carry buckets of steaming water in to fill the tub.

"Would you like me to stay and help with the bath?" Heka offers.

"I can help her," War answers for us both. Heka smiles knowingly and then follows the men out.

War feels the water in the tub before dumping in a bucket of cool water to adjust the temperature. I truly will never underestimate the usefulness of indoor plumbing again. Once he is satisfied that the water will not burn me, War picks me up and carries me to the tub, slowly lowering me into the water. My wounds sting as they meet the warm water, but I breathe through my teeth, knowing that this needs to happen.

Once I am fully submerged, I realize that he left my shirt on—probably offering me a bit of privacy. But I feel like we have firmly crossed that line already, so I pull it off up over my head.

I hear a sharp intake of breath when War sees my entire naked body up close for the first time. Technically he did see me while in his wolf form, but this is different. I know that he can see me. I chose this.

Grabbing the soap and a cloth, War begins washing me. He massages my sore muscles as he cleans the grime from the day off of my skin, turning my arms and back into Jello.

When directed to, I tip my head back and he washes my hair, massaging my scalp and working through any tangles that he finds. I usually try to keep my curls tamed—either by straightening them or keeping them in a braid. Since I have been here, my hair has been left wild.

After my hair is washed, he moves on to the legs, avoiding my sore thighs. Picking up my foot and holding it out of the water, he looks closely at my calf.

"Do you not grow hair here?" he asks. "It is much shorter than I would expect."

I chuckle. "I usually shave the hair off of my legs with a razor, or wax. It is a common thing in my world. I had treated myself to a wax as part of my pre-birthday pampering before I ended up here."

"Do you shave anywhere else?" he asks while taking a closer look at my body.

"Under my arms," I reply. "Some women shave their pussy too—but I like to just keep it neat and trimmed." This is definitely not a conversation that I ever thought I would have with a man—but his curiosity is so genuine. He is always trying to learn something new about me and it makes me feel seen in a way I haven't ever felt before.

His eyes go wide. "Does your species not like hair? It does not bother us here."

I snort. "I figured that out when I saw you shift into a wolf with hair all over your body."

War chuckles at my joke.

"You must shave too." I reach up and hold my hand to his cheek. "If you didn't, I would think that your face would be just as hairy as your wolf's."

"I do. Would you like me to shave you?"

"Um, I would feel more comfortable having my legs shaved but you don't have to..."

He pulls my leg out of the water, rubs it down with soap, and then grabs a knife from the shelf and carefully runs it across my skin. He stops mid-thigh and then repeats the process. Shocked at what he is doing, I just sit there and watch him as he meticulously shaves my legs for me. He tells me that one of his brothers shaves a part of his head. Thinking back to all of the people I met, many sported various facial and hair styles.

After my legs are to his liking—or I guess, my liking—he lifts my arms up and shaves my pits too.

I cannot help the giggle that erupts from my chest when he nods, proud of his work. He looks at me like I am crazy—my giggle turning into a full belly laugh. I should probably calm myself down but seriously, what is my life right now? I just rode on the back of a wolf, all day, through a forest that does not exist in my world. Then, I was washed, massaged, and shaved by the man that the wolf turns into sometimes. Oh, also, he is my soulmate.

"I'm sorry," I say when I have calmed down enough to speak again, "I think that this entire world hopping, being shaved by my wolf shifter Mate thing just got to me. Thank you for helping me."

He smiles. "Hopefully you are still thanking me when I tell you about how I can help you heal even faster."

"Do you have some kind of magic juju that you haven't told me about yet?" He pulls me out of the tub and carefully dries me off before carrying me to the bed.

"I don't know what 'juju' means—but wolves do have magic. It wouldn't be possible to shift without it."

"Huh. I never actually put that together." I admit. "Okay, well lay it on me, Big Guy. What super special healing wolfy powers do you have?"

"My saliva can heal superficial wounds."

That can't... he can't mean that he needs to lick me... right? My clit starts throbbing at the thought of his tongue on my thighs.

"So, you would..." flicking my eyes from his mouth to my thighs, he starts to nod.

"I would use my tongue on you," he confirms.

"And is that something you would be willing to do for me?" My voice comes out much squeakier than I had planned.

"If given the opportunity, I would love to lick every inch of your body—but I will keep my focus on your thighs until you ask for more."

"And if I do? Want more?"

He lowers his voice, half growling in a tone that does some very not PG things to me. "Then I will heal your legs before moving on to that pretty pussy, drinking your pleasure directly from the source."

Am I drooling? God, I want that so bad. It has been so long since I have had a decent orgasm, I need it.

"Please, War," I beg.

He pounces. Spreading my thighs wide open, I am completely exposed to him as he pulls my hips so that I am on the edge of the bed while he kneels on the floor in between my legs. He treats my thighs gently. Licking at them with slow and steady strokes.

I am embarrassingly wet from the attention. He is literally just trying to heal me right now but having his tongue so close to where I really need him has me dripping.

I hear a rumble come from his throat as he smells my arousal.

I don't know if it is from his magic spit or because a different part of me is throbbing—needing attention— but my legs really do start feeling better.

After about 20 minutes, he must feel confident that I am on my way to healing because he looks up. I am so desperate, I let out a whine.

"Please, War. I need you." I reach for him, pulling him by his hair to my pussy. He doesn't hesitate. He dives right in, licking me from ass to clit. He flicks his tongue over my clit, sending pulses of pleasure right through me. "Fuck," I moan.

His finger starts to work me while he spears his tongue into my opening, moaning at the taste. He fucks me with his tongue until I see stars. My entire body spasms as I come. He works me through my orgasm and after I come down from that high, he flips me over, positioning me to kneel at the edge of the bed.

I snort. Of course he would want to do doggy style.

I just had the best orgasm of my life, nothing else has ever come close, so I am game for whatever he has in mind next. Showing my interest, I give my ass a little wiggle at him.

He gives me a light spank, causing me to let out a little yelp. He chuckles and positions himself behind me. But instead of feeling the head of his cock, his fingers breach my core. Pumping them in and out, he adds his tongue back into the mix.

It feels so good that I shamelessly grind my pussy back against his face. I can feel his laugh as it vibrates against my sensitive skin. It is a good thing that War enjoys my eagerness because I am quickly turning into a needy ho—I need this next orgasm more than I have ever needed anything. I am not even sure if it is possible, but he continues working me towards another mind-blowing release. With his fingers pumping in and out of me, he wraps his lips around my clit and sucks, causing wave after wave of pure pleasure to blast through me.

I am so sensitive, I am shaking, but he doesn't stop. I look over my shoulder and watch him move his tongue from my swollen clit up to my asshole. His tongue rims me in slow, smooth circles. I should probably be embarrassed by the sounds coming out of my mouth at this point, but I am too far gone to really care.

I have never had a partner give me multiple orgasms. I have never had a partner touch me there—let alone taste me.

I can feel him shifting and realize that he is jacking himself off while finger fucking my pussy and eating my ass like it is his last meal. This is by far the hottest thing that I have ever experienced. I don't think that there is any way that I could possibly come again after the two Earth shattering orgasms that I have already had, but then I hear him grunt out his release as he works his tongue into my asshole.

I detonate. I scream. I nearly blackout. I would think that I have died and come back to life a new woman, if not for the steady lapping of War's tongue as he drinks the arousal gushing out of me. Not a drop is wasted.

I collapse onto the bed. It has never felt like that before. War crawls to lay over top of me. He takes his soaked finger and paints my lips with it. My tongue licks out to have a taste and I realize that it is not *my* cum that he has given me, but his. I moan as I suck his finger clean.

Releasing his finger from my mouth, I drag his head down and crash my lips to his. He deepens the kiss, exploring my mouth with his tongue, swallowing my moans, and making me breathless when we finally part. I have never been kissed like that before either. Everything with this man is new. Exciting. Perfect. I am nervous that this actually *is* some bizarre dream, and I will wake up, never being satisfied again.

After we catch our breath, War gets up and washes his hands and face with some fresh water. He uses a small wet cloth to clean me up a bit, and then gently places the balm from Heka on my thighs. He feeds me from a tray that someone must have left outside our door—I will probably feel self-conscious about that later—before adding another log to the fire and snuggling into bed with me.

I lay my head on his chest and fall asleep to the steady sound of his heart beating.

Chapter Eight

I wake the next morning with a start. Rowan is not lying in bed next to me. I look around the tent and find it empty. Thinking that she may have needed to relieve herself, I go in search of her. My panic grows when I do not find her.

Focusing on the pull connecting our souls, I follow the thread. It is faint, which means she is close. Not wanting to startle anyone, I try to keep calm as I walk quickly between lodgings. Then, I hear it. Her laugh. A sound that sparks fire in my soul.

Getting closer, I see Rowan sitting with Heka and a few other females from the pack. They are eating breakfast and mending some clothing. When she sees me, she gives me a shy smile. I walk up to her and pull her into my arms, burying my face into her neck and scenting her. She squirms and looks around, possibly feeling shy to be shown such a public display—but everyone can smell me on her anyway.

"Please do not ever leave me asleep in bed again. I was worried about you," I whisper in her ear.

Lifting up onto her toes, she pulls my head down to meet her, pressing her lips to mine in a gentle kiss.

"I'm sorry Big Guy; I was hungry and didn't want to wake you."

Sitting down next to Heka, I pull Rowan into my lap and start feeding her. The need to provide for my Mate overpowers any additional need to mark her further with my scent.

"How are your legs this morning?"

Rowan blushes, pulling a smirk out of me. "Much better. Thank you." She gives me another kiss on my cheek and then turns her attention back to the story that Heka is telling. I continue to hold and feed her until she tells me that she is full.

After breakfast, the mending is packed up and everyone except for Heka goes their different ways. Everyone within the pack has duties to fulfil.

"So, what is the plan for the day? The full moon is tomorrow, right?" Rowan asks, looking to both me and Heka for confirmation.

"Yes, it is." I reply. "I have several things to get done today so I was thinking that you might enjoy working with Heka. She always has patients to see and medicines to make. I am sure she could use your help."

Rowan looks over at Heka who watches us with unveiled delight. "I would love to learn from you, Heka," Rowan says to her.

"And I would love your company, child."

Standing, I pull Rowan flush against my body and tilt her chin up to look me in the eyes. "You are safe here but please stay with Heka. I need to meet with Zeke and then there are some things that I need to attend to just outside the outpost. I will feel better knowing that you are with her while I am gone."

"I promise."

"Good girl." I kiss her, deep and slow. Claiming her for all to see and appeasing my wolf's possessiveness. With one final thrust of my tongue, I pull my mouth from hers—holding her body to mine until the haze of lust clears from her eyes.

Walking with Heka and Rowan until they reach the infirmary, I continue on to meet with Zeke, grabbing some breakfast for myself along the way. Several pack members stop me, making requests and, in some cases, kissing my ass. I try to make sure that everyone is happy, but there are always those who think that they will get more if they dish out compliments. Grumbling to myself as a she-wolf named Dreena rubs up against my legs, I quickly continue on to my meeting with Zeke.

Typically, when we arrive at a village, I make sure that everyone is able to find lodging and help to get everyone settled. I also meet with the pack members who stay in the settlement full time. There are six families that stay at this outpost permanently. And those meetings are usually straightforward—the wolves supplying hunting reports and a list of requested items to be brought with the next supply.

Because I needed to attend to Rowan last night, Zeke took over my responsibilities, and I want to make sure everything went smoothly. There is also a special project that I have planned. I sent a message ahead of time to the local pack families in hopes that they will be able to help me.

I find Zeke discussing hunting routes with some of our hunters. "Good morning," I greet. They all look up and offer me their greetings in return.

"How is Rowan feeling this morning?" Zeke asks.

"Much better. She is working with Heka today while she finishes healing."

Zeke nods and we continue talking about routes and future plans for hunts. The prey seem to be moving in different patterns and we are not sure why. Changes in the weather seem to be happening earlier this year than most. There is still plenty of game, but it is something to keep an eye on.

"I sent a message home letting your brothers know that we will be returning in the next couple of weeks. I didn't say anything about Rowan. I thought you might want to tell them about your Mate yourself."

"I appreciate that, thank you."

"Speaking of your Mate—the full moon is tomorrow night. Have you prepared Rowan for the ceremony? If she is not from here, it is unlikely that she will know what to expect."

"We have discussed it a bit. We do not really know how the bonding will affect her because she does not have a wolf."

"She will still need to bite you, even with her dull teeth," he reminds me. "And there is the matter of what she will wear...and what happens after the ceremony."

"I don't want to make her uncomfortable."

"Which is why you should tell her in advance."

"You are right. I will talk to her tonight."

We locate a group of local pack, mostly females, that will help with my special project. Rowan told me a little bit about weddings, which is something that they have in their world to join two people together through a commitment to each other. I really want to make this bonding nice for her.

Knowing that the ceremony preparations will be taken care of, I pack up a sled with supplies and head out to work on my next project.

I stay out until after the sun has set, returning to the village as most are finishing up dinner. Opening the door to Heka's tent, I am stopped by how beautiful my Mate is. Her golden hair shines in the firelight as she laughs and rolls bandages with Heka.

Rowan makes eye contact with me when she hears me walk in. Her eyes are intense and hold yearning. It was so difficult for me to keep my distance today, but I know it will be worth it tomorrow during our bonding.

"Have you eaten?" I ask.

"Yes. Heka and I had a lovely dinner," she replies. Yawning, she stands and stretches. She is back to only wearing my shirt and the hem rises as she raises her arms above her head, giving me a peek at her delicious thighs.

Last night was the best I have ever had. I had never used my mouth on another before—my wolf would not tolerate the taste of someone other than our Mate—as if he knew that we would find her one day.

My sexual experience has solely been quick fucks to sate a need. In my 107 years, there has never been a short supply of willing bedmates. Both males and females like the idea of being chosen by the Alpha. But to me, they were always only holes to be used. Never more.

Last night was so much more.

I found my release two times at the mere taste of my Mate. I want so badly to give her my knot, and I hope that after we bond, her body will accommodate it. But, if she is never able to take it, I will be satisfied to only hold her for the rest of our lives. I will eagerly accept any part of her that she gives me.

We say goodnight to Heka and walk back to our lodging on the other side of the village, greeting pack members and laughing as pups run from their parents to circle our feet.

"I had so much fun with Heka today," she says.

"Good. I am glad that she is here with us on this trip. She does not usually travel with hunting parties, but she said that her wolf needed to get out and run."

"She taught me about different plants that are used to make medicine. I even found a couple of plants that are similar to what we have in my world. New York is a big city, so I didn't have my own space for a garden, but I volunteered at community gardens when I was able. Plants are so much fuller and brighter here."

"We have space for gardens back at the lodge. You are welcome to plant whatever you like once we get settled."

Arriving at our lodging, my wolf sends me into high alert. Scenting the air, a growl rumbles from my chest. I hold Rowan behind me as we enter.

Kneeling on our bed, fully prone with her ass in the air, is Dreena—the unmated pack member that has been trying to insert herself into my orbit this entire trip.

I hear Rowan gasp behind me. Her hand shaking as she presses it against my back.

"What are you doing here?" I demand with a growl.

She looks over her shoulder, rolling her eyes when she sees Rowan behind me. "Making sure you know you have better options. I am available and yet you choose to Mate with this non-shifter? She is weak. She nearly died from wounds that pups would be able to heal from. She cannot hunt with the pack. She did not even notice the young vakusa that I led to her until after the mother nearly trampled her."

"You led the vakusa pup away from the herd?" I growl, so loudly that the air vibrates around me. "You intentionally put my Mate in danger?"

Dreena scoffs. "She cannot even travel with us as a pack—she was hurt from one day of travel. I will let you breed me right now. I can take your knot better than she ever could. You know that I will always be a better fuck."

"Get. Out."

With one final look at me, she turns to get off the bed. "You are trapped under her spell. You know that I am the better choice. You know that I can offer you things that she never could."

"Get. The. Fuck. Out."

"I have put in my time—joining your pack, working my way onto your hunting parties as a healer. You chose me to accompany you on this trip. You could have chosen any wolf, but you chose me. I am the only unmated female in this hunting party besides Heka. It is obvious that you did that because you wanted me to warm your bed. I know it. Everyone in this outpost knows it. And now I am pushed aside because a non-shifter appeared? I refuse to let that happen. I am your mate. Mate with me now and I will forgive you for this lapse in judgement."

Tears rim her eyes, but I am left totally unaffected by her sadness. She intentionally put my Mate in danger with the vakusa. She may have even given Rowan the wrong medicine on purpose. My wolf is trying to break free—wanting to eliminate this threat to our Mate before Rowan is actually hurt. But we still have many days of travel before we return home so I need to treat this situation with care.

One thing that I can do—must do—is make my intentions clear. Dreena has been speaking in our native language, purposefully, so that Rowan cannot understand what is being said. That stops now. Speaking in Rowan's language, I keep my voice firm. "I have not misled you and I have *never* chosen you. You were selected by Zeke to come on this hunt because you had made it known that you wanted to learn more about healing and wanted to see more of the territory. If you thought that I would allow an unmated female to join our hunting party just so that I had a bedmate, you are sorely mistaken."

Dreena shakes her head in disbelief as she walks closer to the door. But instead of leaving, Dreena shifts and lunges towards Rowan. My wolf tears through my skin, catching Dreena mid-air and slamming her to the ground, but not before Rowan is knocked backwards, hitting her head as she falls.

I shift back and hold Dreena's neck and body with my knees, pinning her to the floor. "Shift back," I order with my Alpha dominance. Her wolf whimpers and I can feel her shaking before she shifts back into her skin.

"ZEKE!" I roar as loud as I can. I do not know where he is in the camp, but he will hear me. I am too angry to use enough control to communicate through my wolf.

Zeke enters a moment later, quickly taking in the scene. Rowan is sitting with her knees pulled to her chest, blood running down her temple, and shaking as she looks at us with wide eyes. I have Dreena pinned by her neck to the ground with my knee, limiting her air supply as I shake with fury.

Zeke comes over to me and pulls Dreena up, securing her arms. "Take her to the outpost center. I will be there later to make a few things clear. Spread the word. Every pack member besides Mated females and children must attend."

Zeke nods and pulls Dreena out of the tent behind him.

Slowly walking over to Rowan, I pull her hands from her face. Her cheeks are wet with tears and blood. Her eyes are red from crying. She looks terrified as she stares at the spot where Dreena just vacated.

"You are safe," I tell her, checking over her wound. Sitting down next to her, Rowan lets me pull her onto my lap. She straddles me and rests her face on my chest. I can feel her blood coating my skin as I rub her back and encourage her to take calming breaths.

"I knew that she didn't like me," she says quietly, "but I never thought that she would try to attack me."

"What makes you say that?" I ask. "Has she treated you unkindly before?" Zeke and I had noticed some of her odd behavior but did not think that it was anything to reprimand urgently. If I had known that she was making Rowan feel uncomfortable, I would have sent her away immediately.

"Not really. But she walked away when I tried introducing myself. And then today, she was watching me as I worked with Heka. She was whispering to some of the other women but whatever she wanted from them, they turned her down. I just thought that she didn't like me. Is she your ex or something?"

"No, I have never had relations with Dreena. She has tried to get in my bed several times—though she has never been so bold as to actually get in my bed like she did tonight. I am sorry that she did that and that she hurt you. I should have seen what she was doing sooner."

"You don't need to apologize. You didn't do anything wrong." Rowan pulls her head back so that she can look me in my eyes. "Thank you for protecting me."

I kiss her forehead. "Always. Do you want to know what she said?"

"No. Not right now, at least. Her actions made her opinions about me clear enough."

We stay there, holding each other and breathing the same air for several minutes before she speaks again.

"Do you think others feel the same way? Will they not want me to be a part of the pack because I am human? I mean, someone like her probably is a better choice for you. I don't have any powers, and we don't know for sure that we are, um, compatible."

"There might be some, like Dreena, that are disappointed that I am not available anymore. But True Mates are sacred to us. The pack will accept you because I am their Alpha and you hold my soul. There is not anyone else for me. There has always only been you. Even before I met you. You are mine, just as I am yours."

"I don't want to cause issues for you with your pack," she softly confesses.

Bringing my hands to her cheeks, I hold her face gently. "You did not cause what happened here tonight. You are my Mate. That is something that was decided by
109

The Mother during creation, long before any of us were given life. You did not choose to come here. You were brought here by a power so strong that it crossed worlds. What Dreena tried to do tonight would have been unacceptable even if I had yet to find you. To attack you in addition to her pathetic display is an unforgivable offense that will not go unpunished."

I hear a sharp intake of breath. "Please don't kill her," she pleads. "I don't think that I can handle that on my conscience."

Honestly, that had been my plan. My pack needs to know that acts against my Mate will not be tolerated. I grind my teeth as I try to think of an alternative. My wolf is demanding that I rip her throat out. He almost did it the moment she lunged towards Rowan.

"Please War." Despite the fear still coursing through her veins, she keeps her voice soft as she pleads on her attacker's behalf.

I nod my head. If I cannot kill her, then there is only one other option.

"Come with me." I put on a pair of pants and then reach for Rowan, checking her wound to make sure that the bleeding has slowed. I will heal her, but first I want the pack to see visible evidence of the attack. Hand in hand, we walk through the outpost. The pack has been gathered like I instructed. In the center, Dreena kneels. Her hands have been tied with leather straps and Zeke stands guard. When they see us, everyone quiets. Rowan tries to pull away from me to stand with Heka, but I keep her at my side where she belongs. She takes a deep breath, squares her shoulders, and faces the crowd as I speak.

"Tonight, a grave offense was made against my Mate. In a pitiful attempt to seduce me away from sealing the bond with my True Mate, Dreena snuck into our lodging while we were away and laid in presentation on our bed. This act, while odious on its own, was made worse when Dreena shifted and lunged towards Rowan's neck, but not before she confessed to other failed attempts to endanger my Mate.

"As you know, my wolf is the judge, juror, and executioner of this pack. My wolf calls for death."

There is a gasp in the crowd, but nobody steps forward to challenge my ruling. I wait for a moment, making sure that they all understand the severity of her actions.

"My Mate, however, is more forgiving than my wolf. Tomorrow, under the full moon, my True Mate and I will become one. She will rise to be my equal in all ways—with or without a wolf of her own. Because we do not wish to start our union with bloodshed, we will rule with leniency. But, make no mistake, any further acts of violence against my Mate will be dealt with by brutal force.

Turning back to face her, I say, "Dreena, you are banished from the Nightfang pack. You may try to join Nightfury or Nighthowl, but they will be informed of your betrayal. If you are turned away by my brothers, you will leave all three territories as a lone wolf. You will have three days to leave my territory. If you return, you will be put to death. I suggest you run."

Dreena glares at me while I announce her sentence but does not try to deny the claims.

As soon as Zeke unties the leather bindings around her wrists, Dreena snarls as she shifts back into her dark wolf and runs into the quiet forest, away from our pack. My wolf severs the pack bond between us, and we all hear the pained howl as she runs away. Several wolves whimper at the sound. Even if they agree with my ruling, severing a pack bond is heartbreaking for a wolf. The only cure for such pain is finding your place within another pack—an option that is unlikely for Dreena.

Addressing my pack once more, I say "Get some rest. Tomorrow is the full moon and a cause for celebration. Any pack members with children who would like to participate in tomorrow night's festivities, please speak with Heka. She will be coordinating care for the pups."

With that, I scoop Rowan into my arms and lick at her wound as I walk back to our tent.

"I can walk, you know," she whispers.

"I know. But I need to touch you right now," I explain. Rowan smiles and tucks her head against my neck.

I rip the top layers of bedding off of our bed when we get back, getting rid of anything that has Dreena's scent. Putting them outside to be washed or destroyed—I could not care less—I return to my Mate's side.

"Zeke reminded me today that there is more that we should discuss about the ceremony tomorrow..."

"I spoke to Heka about it a little bit today. But I do have some questions."

Stripping us both out of our clothes, I tuck us into bed and pull her close so that her head is resting on my arm while I lay on my side. My hard cock nudges her side. "Ignore that." She giggles. "What are your questions?"

"Will your bite hurt? You have to break the skin, right? Will you be you or all wolfy?"

I chuckle. "I don't know if it will hurt or not. For wolves, it causes pleasure—it might feel different for humans. But my saliva will heal it almost instantly. It will leave a scar to show that you are claimed. I will have one too from where you bite me."

"When I what? I can't bite you. I don't have wolf teeth. Look at these things," she shows me her teeth, "they aren't sharp at all. They can't even bite through steak without outside help."

"You can bite me, and you will. It needs to be done to complete the bond. You will just need to bite me harder than I bite you."

"But I don't have magic juju spit. And I'm not a vampire. No offense, but I really have zero desire to drink your blood."

A loud laugh barrels out of me. "I will heal just fine without it. You will taste my blood when you bite, but you do not need to suck me dry like a leech."

"Well, sucking you dry is something that I can get behind." She winks suggestively and then cackles as I tickle her. After she catches her breath, she asks, "Is there anything else that I should know?"

"Just a few things," I reply.

We talk until she cannot keep her eyes open any longer. Wrapping her tight in my arms, I hold her while she sleeps. I know that she is nervous for tomorrow but there is excitement too. I close my eyes, feeling damn lucky that I am holding my forever in my arms.

Chapter Nine

I am freaking the fuck out. Like, breathing into a paper bag, can't hear anything over the blood rushing in my ears, body feels itchy level freaking. Heka is helping me get ready for the bonding ceremony and I am about 20 seconds away from a full-blown panic attack.

I have been scrubbed and lathered in oils. My hair has been left mostly wild but pulled back from my face with a few intricate braids. This is as close as I am ever going to get to a wedding ceremony—Heka even gave me a sex talk, which is an hour of my life that I will never get back. I can't help but wish my sisters were here to help me through this. I'm trying to not let it bum me out, so I hold them in my heart as I allow Heka to fuss with my hair. Ramsey would use her no-nonsense attitude to lay all of the facts out in front of me. She would want me to make a pros and cons list for whether this is the right choice to make. I would tell her that there is no choice. It is fate. She would eventually give in. Reese would gush about how I am living in a fairy tale, complete with my own beastly prince. Her cheeks would flame red when I blurted out, in great detail, all the ways that War rocked my world the other night. We would joke around, and it would all distract me from the very real fact that I am about to walk naked through a pack of near strangers.

Heka just presented me with my outfit. I knew that this was coming. I just don't think that it fully set in when War told me last night. My outfit for the ceremony contains four jeweled cuffs. Two for my wrists and two for my ankles. They are beautiful, truly. About four inches wide. Made from a polished metal and then adorned with natural stones and gems. Each unique but matching at the same time.

That is my wedding attire in its entirety. Four cuffs.

I am to walk through the pack, naked, to seal the bond with my Mate under the full moon. War also told me that many Mates choose to physically seal the bond in front of the pack as well—but since it is not required, he has arranged for us to have privacy for that part. You know, the part where we will have sex over and over again for days.

War explained that after we exchange bites, the rest of the pack will basically take part in an orgy, which is why Heka has arranged for the children to be kept away and occupied for the night.

So here I stand, polished and naked, waiting for the ceremony to start where I will bite my soulmate and start a fuck fest under the moon.

I focus on my breathing and remind myself for the thousandth time that nudity is a common thing here. Back in New York, I would never have considered myself modest. I was willing to try most fashion trends as long as it fit the occasion. But my clothing always covered my pussy lips. That was a line I did not cross. I snort to myself. Maybe I am a prude. Maybe I should embrace my inner wolf and let my flaps fly free. Lord. What would Reese think if she saw me right now?

Another deep breath and then I push aside my worry about what will happen when some of War's powers are transferred over to me. It is unknown what it will entail, but all previous pairings resulted in a positive exchange. It should make me stronger. Safer. Another deep breath and the door opens.

It is time.

I put on a brave face and start my journey through the village to where the pack is waiting. War told me that often, the pack would be shifted into their wolves—but since that is not an option for me, everyone has chosen to remain out of fur.

It is a gesture that I didn't know I would appreciate as much as I do. Seeing the faces of people, instead of a pack of wolves, shows me that they are accepting of my form. I blink back tears as I see all of their encouraging faces.

I continue on until I am standing before War. He looks at me like I hold his entire world. And maybe I do—because, as crazy as it sounds, that is how I feel about him too.

The bright moon is high in the dark sky, surrounded by twinkling stars. It is so big and brilliant that it works as a spotlight, illuminating the sharp lines and striking features on War's face. Back home, I rarely saw stars. New York is too bright—you have to drive away from the city to find them. But here, they blanket the sky, making the vivid colors in this world sparkle.

War looks up at the sky too. A look of awe washes over his face as if he is seeing it all for the first time. And then he speaks, his voice so low that I do not know if the pack will be able to hear. It is a gentle reminder that while there are witnesses to this ceremony, his words are only for me. "We are taught that The Mother found her soul match with The Moon. Together, they breathed life into the wolves, encouraging us to care for the land as dutifully as we worship the sky. Together, they provide for us as we care for them. Just as we will provide for and take care of each other as True Mates." Bringing my hands up to his face, he gently seals his promise with a kiss on my knuckles.

"Growing up, my sisters and I did not have a family to take care of us. Our parents did not care for us when we were little, so we were moved around to different families that were willing to take us in for a short time. Sometimes, all three of us were able to stay together but most often, we were split up. Whenever we were apart, we would look to the moon to connect us. We knew that no matter how far apart we were, we could all look up and see the same moon. The moon gave us security when the rest of our world couldn't. I would pray to the moon each night, asking for my family to be brought back together."

Feeling shy from my admission and the tears that are leaking down my cheeks, I quickly look away.

Tilting my chin up so that I am forced to meet his eye, War gives me a reassuring smile. "I promise that you will never feel uncared for again. You will always have a home with me." With tears in our eyes, War bends his head to place a soft kiss on my lips. "Maybe your moon and mine brought us together in this world so that we could find each other."

I smile. "And maybe my sisters and your brothers are looking up at the same moon—being here with us even though they are far away."

War nods and kisses my forehead before he continues. "For my entire life, I knew that I would fill the role as Alpha. Living for the pack, providing for it like I knew I would, has always felt like my greatest accomplishment. But from the moment that my wolf caught your trail, my world as I knew it shifted. I still take great pride in my pack, I always will—but being your Mate has filled me with so much joy and purpose that I do not know if I was ever truly living before I met you. We have not known each other for long but I am certain that I want to spend forever getting to know you. You are my True Mate—the keeper of my soul—and I choose you to be mine today, tomorrow, and every day that follows."

The tears in my eyes blur the sharpness of War's handsome face. His blue eyes pull me into depths that I would drown in if he wasn't there to hold me tight. Stretching up onto my toes, I kiss War and with my lips I tell him every feeling that I cannot put words to.

"Are you ready?" he asks, pulling away once we are breathless.

"Almost," I whisper. "Other than my sisters, I have never had someone claim me as theirs. I have always been too loud, too impulsive, too much. But you see me differently. You see me as being exactly how I should be. I want you to know that even though we are still learning about each other, I will always choose you too."

"You are mine, just as I am yours."

I nod and parrot his words back to him. "You are mine, just as I am yours."

War leans in and I feel the sharp pinch of his teeth piercing my skin right where my neck meets my shoulder. My veins feel hot, lava spreading throughout my body and then settling in my chest and core. I feel War's tongue lapping at my wound as he pulls my mouth to his neck. Before I can chicken out, I bite down until I can taste blood, marking him in the same place he marked me. The lava in my core turns into burning desire, more intense than anything I have ever felt before. I moan as he pulls my teeth from his neck and crashes his mouth to mine. I taste my blood on his tongue and deepen the kiss, hungry for his desire as if it is all I could ever need. I rock my hips against him, needing to ease the pressure between my legs.

An instant later, War shifts into his wolf, scooping me up to straddle his back. He takes us away from the pack at a sprint. The friction of his body moving against my clit causes a climax so suddenly that I almost fall from his back.

We are running through the forest for only about ten minutes before we stop in front of a grotto hidden behind a waterfall. War shifts back and walks me to the opening of the cave. Inside the cave is a large bed surrounded by hundreds of candles.

"Did you do all of this?" I ask, momentarily stunned by the beauty.

"I had some help. I wanted tonight to be special for you."

"It's beautiful." Holding his hand, I walk backwards until my legs hit the bed. I pull War down on top of me, wrapping my thighs around his hips. He captures my mouth with his. He is unhurried, as if we have all of the time in the world. And I guess we do.

"I need to be inside of you," he says. "I promise I will be gentler with you next time, okay?"

"Please, War. I don't need gentle. I need to feel you."

I feel the head of War's huge cock nudge my entrance. I am already soaked. He slides in slowly, giving me time to stretch around him. Little by little, he works himself inside of me.

"You take my cock so well, love. Your pussy is gripping me the whole way in." War's fingers dig into my hips, leaving bruises as he holds himself back from pounding into me.

I moan, unsure if I can take anymore of him. I feel so full.

"Just a little more, Sunshine. Your cunt has almost swallowed my entire cock." He rubs my clit, relaxing my muscles just a little more, allowing him to fit the rest of his cock inside of me. I moan again when I feel his pelvis grind against my clit and his balls slap against my ass.

He waits, giving me more time to adjust as he kisses my lips, my neck, and my nipples—sucking them into his mouth. He flicks my tight buds with his tongue and I almost come just from that. Everything feels so sensitive right now, I think a gust of wind could set me off. I adjust my hips, letting him know that I am ready.

War fucks me hard but slow. Each thrust is purposeful, unwavering. Each thrust a promise of what we are now and what we will always be for each other. His hand gently twines in my hair as he grips the back of my neck and brings his forehead down to rest on mine.

His cock reaches a spot inside of me that I didn't even know was there. It is as if my body has been pulled apart and remade to accommodate him. The perfect fit.

Weaving my fingers through his shoulder length hair, I pull his mouth back to mine, needing to seal us together in every way. I flick the tip of his tongue with my own before sucking it into my mouth, like I would if it was his cock in my mouth instead. He moans and I can feel his dick jerk inside me.

With one extra hard thrust, War pushes even further into me, letting his knot expand within my walls. The slow build up of my climax transforms into a release so big that my vision goes dark. I can feel a pulse of electricity in the air and my body convulses. War comes at the same time, shooting ropes of his seed deep within me.

Locked together, the burning that I felt in my chest after the bite spreads outward towards my shoulders. When the warmth cools, I can't help but reach up and trace the intricate design that now adorns War's chest. He does the same to me.

I look down to discover a matching design to War's on my body.

Like a tattoo but with shimmering silver ink, the phases of the moon run shoulder to shoulder across our chests.

"What does this mean?" I ask.

"Moon Touched," he whispers with awe. "I have only heard of this through legend. While all True Mates are given by The Mother, some pairings are also blessed by The Moon. In stories, Moon Touched Mates are unmatched in power and strength. It is the most sacred bonding to exist."

He wipes the tears collecting in my eyes. "Are you okay, love? I did not cause you pain, did I?"

"You didn't hurt me. I'm okay. This just all feels so big—so much bigger than me. I guess I just keep being surprised by the magic of this world. To find my soulmate, to be here with you, at this moment, it's all pretty surreal. I keep thinking that I am going to wake up and this will have been just a dream.

"I'm real, Sunshine. This is real. I'm so lucky to have you in my life. I love you, Rowan."

"I love you too, Warrick." I have never felt more sure of anything in my life.

We lay in each other's arms until War's knot goes down enough for him to pull out. Then, he takes his mouth to my sore pussy, making me come on his tongue before fucking and knotting me again. And again. And again. Best night ever.

Chapter Ten

Rowan

It has been six days of nearly constant fucking. Our cozy grotto has been an amazing place for War and I to enjoy each other without any interruptions, but we do need to head back to the pack and continue with our journey home. We were able to chat a little bit while knotted together and decided that our best chance of finding my sisters, if they are even in this world, is to ask his brothers for help.

War has already sent messages to certain wolves throughout his territory, asking for them to keep an eye out for any non-shifters. We need his brothers to do the same, but War wants to fill them in in person.

After bathing in the pool of water under the waterfall, we make love one last time before heading back to the village. War packed me some clothes with the food that he stored for us in the cave, so I do not need to return in my birthday suit. Climbing up onto the wolf's back, I ride the short distance back through the forest.

At the edge of the village, War shifts back and puts on a pair of pants before grabbing my hand and walking the rest of the way with me on foot. Zeke meets us by the central fire. When he sees the markings on War's bare chest, his eyes go wide.

"Moon Touched?" he asks. "I have only ever heard about this. Do you feel any different?"

"I'm not sure," War replies. "Something feels 'more' but I have not figured it out yet. We have been a little preoccupied."

"I'm sure you have been," Zeke chuckles, a knowing look in his eye. "And what about you, Rowan? Do you feel any different?"

"I feel warmer...and different, but I don't really know how to explain it. We don't think that I have a wolf, though. I don't sense another being—just something else."

"Well, I'm sure everything will reveal itself with time," Zeke says.

"Are we still all set to move on tomorrow?" War asks Zeke.

They continue talking but I zone out, thinking about this feeling of 'other' inside of me. There is no telling what it could be. I do appear to have quicker healing now. I stepped on a sharp rock in the cave and my cut healed quickly. We obviously aren't going to test the limit on that new power, but it should at least help my legs when we travel tomorrow.

We will be riding for two days before we reach the next outpost. I tried explaining to War that I never made a good girl scout. He didn't really understand what I meant but did tell me that I could sleep on top of him so that I am not sleeping on the ground and that he will keep my mouth occupied so that I don't accidentally swallow any bugs.

The mere suggestion of my mouth being occupied earned him a blowjob and the conversation got put on the back burner for another day.

While Zeke continues to catch War up on what he missed while we were away, I make my way over to a group of ladies who are mending some clothes.

"Welcome back," Eden greets with a smile.

"Thank you. Is there anything that I can help with? To be frank, I have never sewn a thing in my life, but I am willing to learn," I offer.

One of the ladies, Joola, hands me a blanket that appears to have some gashes in it. "I will gladly take the help fixing this. My pup threw a tantrum and decided taking his claws to his bedding was a good idea."

I look closely at the blanket and then grab the needle and thin leather binding that she offers. Taking my time, I stitch the rips closed. When I am done with the blanket, a couple of the other ladies give me some items to work on. Nothing comes out perfect, but I am happy to be able to lend a hand.

After a while, War pulls me away from the ladies and we make our way to our tent, grabbing dinner along the way. War must have arranged for water to be brought in because the tub is full of steaming water when we get inside.

"Food or bath first?" I ask.

"Bath," he replies. "You are wearing far too many clothes my love."

"I am only wearing your shirt!"

"Like I said, far too many." He smirks and then lifts his shirt over my head. He quickly rids himself of his pants and then walks me over to the tub. Climbing in first, he lowers himself into the water before helping me to climb in and sit between his legs. He pulls me back so that I am leaning against his chest. This tub is definitely not meant for two—and if I was the size of a wolf shifter, there is no way that we would both fit—but I couldn't care less. Being wrapped in War's arms is one of the best feelings in the whole world.

We sit together, soaking in the moment, before he starts washing me. He washes and detangles my hair before quickly working on his own. He turns me so that my back is resting against the opposite side of the tub, facing him. He holds my legs out of the water and carefully shaves each one.

When he is done with my legs, he pulls me forward to straddle him, raising my arms and ridding my underarms of hair as well. He has somehow turned something as mundane as shaving into an incredibly sexy event. If I wasn't in the tub, I would be dripping down my thighs.

Sensing my desire, he moves me close for a kiss. I pull his tongue into my mouth, just like I know he likes, and suck on it, causing him to moan and his already hard cock to jerk beneath me. He moves his mouth to my nipples, sucking, flicking, and biting at them. I hold his head to my breasts while I grind my pussy against him.

Not wanting to make too much of a mess with the water, he stands—lifting me with him as he climbs out of the tub. He lays me down on some blankets that were warming by the fire. Flipping me to my stomach, War pulls my ass up so that I am on my knees with my face pressed to the ground. He slides into my core in one hard thrust. We both moan as he fills me.

Fucking me fast and hard, he quickly pulls an orgasm from me. Not stopping to allow me to recover, he continues thrusting in and out. I can feel the sharp scrape of his teeth against my spine as he changes his rhythm and angle, hitting me in a new spot as another orgasm starts to build. War brings me closer and closer until he suddenly pulls out, dropping behind me. Propped on my forearms, he lifts my thighs onto his shoulders and brings his mouth to my sensitive clit while spearing two fingers inside of me. Sucking on my clit, another orgasm plows through me.

Putting me back on my knees, he thrusts his cock back into me. I am panting and moaning. It is all too much.

"You are going to give me one more."

"I can't," I whine, tears falling from my eyes at the intensity.

"Yes, you can. Give me one more, love. I want to fill your pussy with my cum."

He takes his fingers that are still wet from fingering my core and pushes them into my ass. He works them in and out in time with his cock. His knot swells as he pushes inside me one last time and I shatter, squeezing his fingers and milking his cock dry.

He carefully pulls his fingers from me and then rolls us over so that we are laying on our sides while we wait for his knot to go down. He kisses my shoulder and holds me close as we both catch our breath.

"Why are you so good at that?" I mumble, exhaustion dragging me under.

"It has only ever been like this with you."

The next morning, I wake with a moan leaving my lips. War is feasting between my legs. I reach down and grab his hair, encouraging his tongue to delve deeper into my folds. War chuckles and then nips at my clit. I come with his name on my lips.

He works his way back up to kiss my lips. His face is glistening with my arousal as he smiles before nuzzling into my neck.

"Good morning, Sunshine."

"We should start every morning that way," I reply. "How long do we have before we need to leave?"

"Not enough time to do what I really want with you," he growls into my ear. He gives my ear a little nibble. I sigh and start to get up. We would end up staying in bed all day if we didn't get up now.

We had packed up our small bag last night before falling into bed together. Because I am able to heal quickly now, and the weather has been unseasonably warm for the last few days, I have decided to not wear the leather pants this time.

Heka has made me a few dresses to wear out of War's shirts. They are still long sleeved, but the fabric is loose and flowy so I won't get too warm. She also gave me a leather harness-like piece that I can wear over the dress to provide support to my breasts. If I had some leather boots to go with it, it would totally be something I could wear back in New York. But, shoes aren't really a thing here. War is going to have some crafted for me when we get back to his home.

Getting dressed, I quickly splash some cold water onto my face and then pull my hair back into a braid, tying it off with a thin piece of leather that War sometimes uses for his own hair. War gets himself cleaned up a bit too but doesn't bother getting dressed. He will shift before leaving the tent.

Food was delivered to our door early this morning, so we quickly eat. With one last kiss, War shifts into his wolf. I kneel and pull the wolf into a hug. I kiss his muzzle and then climb on his back.

The pack greets me as we approach and then we take off.

I spend most of the early morning taking in the scenery. New York has Central Park, of course, but most of the city is filled with concrete and machines. It feels so refreshing to be surrounded by nature. The forest comes alive around us as we run. Everything is greener, blooming, and full of life.

After we stop to take a quick pee break, I climb back up on War's back. I can tell that the kids are feeling a little bored, so I suggest a game of Eye-Spy. The kids are having a blast and honestly, I am too. The first day of travel goes a lot smoother than the last time I was riding all day.

War directs the pack to a small clearing for us to make camp for the night. The pack works together to lay out some bedding for the kids around the fire. We all eat and then find quiet spots to rest for the night.

War pulls me a little further from camp. As soon as we are out of sight, he backs me up against a tree and seals his mouth to mine. He kisses me until I am dizzy.

"You were such a tease all day today rubbing your bare pussy against my wolf's back," he growls in my ear.

"How selfish of me," I reply with a flirtatious smile. "Let me make it up to you." I slide down to my knees, undoing the laces on his pants and pull his cock out. I lick the bead of precum off of his tip and then take him into my mouth. He is far too large to fully fit, so I wrap my hands around the base of his cock and squeeze as I work him into my mouth. When he hits the back of my throat, a growl rumbles from his chest. I smile around his cock and then swallow him down further.

"Are you going to drink my seed like a good girl?" he asks.

I moan around him and work him over and over, swirling my tongue around his head. I can feel his knot start to swell in my hand so I suck him as deep into my throat as I can while squeezing his knot hard. He comes instantly, cursing and then praising me with his filthy mouth.

War pulls me back up to stand and licks his cum off of my chin before slamming his mouth onto mine. Still hard, he picks me up by the thighs and impales me with his cock in one motion. He fucks me hard against the tree, holding his hand over my mouth to stifle my moans. There is no doubt that the pack can still hear us, but we do not want to wake the kids up.

I can feel my pussy fluttering around War's cock as my orgasm builds. War pinches my clit as his knot expands within me. He gently bites down on my Mate mark, and I scream out my release into War's shoulder. He continues to rut into me until the waves of my orgasm fizzle out.

Turning us around so that his back is to the tree, he slides us down to sit. I straddle War's lap and snuggle in tight to his chest as he wraps his arms around me. Warm and relaxed, I fall asleep knotted to my Mate.

War wakes me up early the next morning with gentle kisses to my face. I look around and realize that we never made it back to the camp last night. We are still up against the tree.

"I'm so sorry," I say. "I didn't mean to fall asleep like that last night."

"You have nothing to apologize for. You are welcome to fall asleep while strangling my cock any time. In fact, I encourage it. Let's always fall asleep with me in you," he says with a smile.

I giggle. While it seems a bit impractical, I really did sleep well last night. Maybe we are onto something.

War and I reluctantly untangle ourselves and head back to the camp. We quickly eat and then head out for another long day of travel. If all goes to plan, we should arrive at our next stop around nightfall.

Chapter Eleven

Running through the forest, the trees and plants are all looking incredibly healthy. As the Alpha, it is important to take notice of any changes in the environment to make sure that we do not overhunt or impact the natural cycles in a negative way.

The air is warmer here than it typically is this time of year. It is as if the growing season is arriving earlier than it should. I will need to talk to my brothers to see if they are seeing similar trends.

While we travel, I try to open my mental link with Rowan. Now that we are fully Mated, I can feel her thread in my wolf's mind, but something is blocking the pathway to communicate. It is possible that it will remain blocked since she does not have a wolf. But, I am hoping that it is something we will be able to develop over time. Our souls require us to be physically close to each other, but my wolf would feel more settled if we could always communicate, despite any distance between us.

Stopping as we near the village, I can already feel that something is off within the pack. There is tension coming through the pack bond that makes my hackles raise. Shifting, I quickly reach out to hold Rowan so that she does not fall. I quickly dress and then pull Rowan into a hug.

"Something is wrong," I whisper into her ear. "Stay close. Zeke will walk with us." Rowan tenses in my arms before subtly nodding.

There are only two families that live at this outpost. I reach out through the pack bond to notify them of our approach. Both males reply, telling me that they have not yet returned from hunting this evening but that their partners were prepared for our arrival.

As we enter the village, fires are lit and it appears that lodgings have been opened for our party, but the typical greeting that I would expect does not meet us. Scenting the air, I know that there are two females and

one pup that have been moving about the camp recently—
but I am not sure where they are now.

"Zeke, go with Heka in search of the females. Make
sure that everyone is healthy. They should have been here
to greet us."

While they split off, Rowan helps entertain the
pups while I assign everyone to their tents. Food has not
been prepared for our arrival either, so we work together
to find, cook, and dish out dinner while sitting around the
central fire.

"All of this should have been done prior to our
arrival," I grumble as Rowan sits down next to me.

"Do you think everything is okay?" Rowan asks
quietly.

I tuck her into my side. "This outpost is not used to
parties our size, but they should have still been here to
greet us and provide food."

"Was everyone able to find what they will need? I
helped Eden and Joola make beds for the kids from what
we brought with us, but it didn't look like much else was
done in the tents other than preparing fires."

"Yes. The single hunters will need to sleep grouped
up, but we were expecting that. They will have to work to
refill the food stores after we leave. There should be
plenty of game in the area."

"If there is enough game, why are their stores so low?"

"I am not sure. It could be that they had recent visitors pass through. I will need to speak to the local hunters to make sure that there is not a bigger issue."

Zeke and Heka return about an hour later.

"Everyone is healthy," Heka reports, her jaw ticking with irritation.

"Where are they?" asks Rowan.

"The females are remaining in their homes with the pup. They do not wish to come out." Zeke gives me a look, and I know he wishes to say more. The four of us move out of earshot from the pack.

"Dreena came through here a few days ago before crossing over into Nighthowl land," Zeke explains. "She told them that you have Mated with a witch, an evildoer who will steal their magic and bring the end of the Nightfang pack."

"What? That is ridiculous. I'm not a witch! I am just a barista and amateur gardener." The unshed tears in her eyes betray the hurt that she tries to hide. She looks around at the half set up outpost. "This is because of me?"

"Dreena has twisted them up in fear. They believe that a wolf who mates with a non-wolf does not deserve the respect given an Alpha," Heka adds with a snarl.

I see red.

"If they do not respect me as an Alpha, then they can get out of my fucking territory," I growl. Ro swipes at her cheeks, clearing the tears that have fallen. "None of this is your fault, sweetheart. I should have had a wolf escort her out of our territory."

Rowan presses her face to my chest, wrapping her arms tightly around my middle. "We need to wait until their partners return. There is a pup involved, War."

Taking a steadying breath, I turn to Zeke. "Put guards outside their doors. They do not leave their homes without permission. We will address them when their partners return."

Picking up Rowan, I carry her over to our lodging. This village, being one of our smaller outposts, only has a few semi-permanent structures. One of them belongs to me, just like in every outpost in my territory. I keep each of them stocked with personal items so that I do not need to bring anything with me while traveling.

Walking through the door, an uncontrolled growl rumbles up through my chest.

The fire ring is cold, and no wood has been gathered. The bed is gone. There are no blankets or furs. My trunk is empty—extra clothing missing. The tub is without soaps or furs for drying. This is not just the insult of the camp not being prepared for us—someone has emptied it of my belongings.

Rowan is looking around the room with tears in her eyes once more as she comes to the same conclusion I have. This was done so that we would feel unwelcome in our own home.

"I am so sorry, love. You deserve so much more than this." I pull my Mate into a hug. "We will find somewhere else to stay tonight."

"I don't need anything fancy," she says quietly into my chest. "I just need you. I'm just sorry that I have caused issues within the pack."

I hold her face in my palms, not wanting her to miss a single word. "This is not your fault. You did not do anything to cause this. You are my Mate. My Moon Touched, True Mate. I love you, Ro. If there are members of my pack that can be so easily turned against me, then they do not belong in my pack. The disrespect that was shown to us tonight is not acceptable."

Rowan and I leave our tent in search of some bedding for the night.

We make our way through the camp. Truthfully, I would not normally stop here with a hunting party our size, but it is in the most direct route toward home. Families with pups always get their own space, when available. Single hunters are usually able to have their own as well, but here they are all doubled or tripled up. There is not an extra tent to stay in and the bedding that was removed from our tent is nowhere to be found.

Exhausted after our long day of travel, I sit down by the central fire and drag Rowan into my lap. The ground is not going to be any less comfortable here than back in our empty home, but there is at least a warm fire here.

Rowan falls asleep in my arms. I feel her shiver from the cool night air and hold her a little tighter. My wolf is angry, wanting to find whoever was responsible for taking comfort away from our Mate. Rowan might not have a wolf, but she is my queen. She deserves the respect of our pack.

Knowing that I will not sleep tonight, I contact my brothers. While communicating with my brothers mind to mind is similar to communication with my pack, it is not something that everyone can do. Because of our bond as brothers, and our joint roles as Alpha, we are tethered. Once we selected our Betas, we learned that a similar tether formed between them as well. Communicating this way can drain our magic quicker and can cause headaches, but it is a useful skill when we spend so much time apart.

"Bade. Griff. Wake your asses up. I have a lot to catch you up on," I say through my wolf. I chuckle when I hear Bade's growl in my head.

"Did I interrupt a good dream, brother?" I ask.

"You interrupted a good orgasm," he grumbles.

"Sorry. But this is more important. Tell your plaything to leave. I need you to focus. Griff, are you with us?"

"I'm here," he replies. *"I fell asleep at my desk again, so I am actually grateful for the wakeup call."*

"I'm glad that one of you appreciates me," I reply.

"What is so important that you need to bug me in the middle of the night?" asks Bade.

"My Mate and I will be arriving home soon. Most likely tomorrow as long as issues at this outpost can be resolved."

"I'm sorry," Griff chimes in, *"did you say Mate?"*

"Yes. I have found my True Mate. We bonded under the full moon. I was planning on telling you in person, but we have run into some issues, and I need to

make you both informed of a few things." I can feel their shock through the bond.

"First, my Mate is from a different world entirely. We do not know how. She is not a shifter. She calls herself a human."

"What the fuck?" Bade grumbles.

"How is this possible?" Griff questions.

"We do not have answers to that. It just is. She has sisters who might have been sent here as well. Please keep an ear out for them within your packs. They are not used to living off of the land and could be in danger by themselves."

"Noted." Bade is clearly not appreciative of me interrupting his activities tonight.

"Griff, a wolf named Dreena was banished from my pack several days ago. She attacked my Mate out of jealousy. She has made it into your territory where she might ask to join your pack. Do what you must, but my wolf will rip out her throat if we ever see her again. She has been spouting hate for my Mate, accusing her of being a witch, and convincing wolves at outposts that she will bring the end to the Nightfang pack. My lodging at the outpost we are currently at has been ransacked. I am holding Rowan as she sleeps by the central fire tonight."

"She will be found and turned away," Griff states.

"Is that all?" ask Bade.

"Just one more thing," I say. "Rowan came to me with no magic. Yet, when we bonded and received our Moon Touched markings—"

"Your what? You are Moon Touched?" I can feel both of their shock as Griff's words interrupt me.

"Yes. And we have since noticed a few things. She can heal quicker, which we expected. She does not appear to have a wolf or any other form to shift into. But she can feel a sense of something more within her. Reaching through our bond, I can feel it too. I have not been able to link my mind with hers yet, but there is something there."

"From what I have read, it can take some time for the powers to fully present themselves after a bonding," Griff explains. "But Moon Touched magic is so rare. That could be what she is feeling within herself. I have never heard of a True Mate pairing involving a non-shifter, but it is clearly possible. I can look into it more for you."

"That would be great. There is one more thing that has been concerning me. Is it unseasonably warm in your territories?"

"No," Bade replies. "Much of my territory still contains ice and snow, though the thaw should be starting soon."

"No changes in weather here. Why do you ask?" asks Griff.

"In the last few days, I have noticed an increase in temperature during the day. Even the nights, while still cool, are tolerable. While we travel through the forest, the land seems to flourish. Leaves are greener and flowers are starting to bloom. It is like they are waking up in our presence. I think...I do not know for sure, but I think that Ro might be making it happen without even knowing it. I asked a wolf at the outpost that we left two days ago about the weather today and he said that while it had been warm when we were there, it cooled back down to normal temperatures since we left."

"Usually, a True Mate bond would only copy some of your traits and pass them over to her. But it is possible that it is a Moon Touched gift. Or maybe she had unknown magic that was unlocked during the ceremony...I have some texts that I will check." Out of the three of us, Griffin is the most book smart. If there is an answer to all of this, he will find it in his library.

"Get some sleep brothers. I will see you soon."

The hunters return an hour later. When they see their homes guarded, they start to panic. I make them wait with the guards, unable to go inside where their families sleep comfortably, and watch as I hold my Mate out in the open by the fire all night long.

Based on their reaction to seeing the guards, I am not sure if they were involved or even aware of the disrespect that we were shown. Hard choices will be made tomorrow—and I doubt they will like their options.

Chapter Twelve

Rowan

I open my eyes just as the sun is starting to color the sky in beautiful shades of pinks and oranges. Looking at his face, I can tell that War hasn't slept. He must be exhausted after so much travel, but I know that his need to protect me and provide for me outweigh his ability to sleep.

I pull his lips to mine and run my tongue along the crease in his lips. He opens for me, and I suck his tongue into my mouth. Our kiss is languid, sleepy—but not any less passionate. He turns our bodies a little bit and then snakes his hand under my dress. I sneak my hands under his shirt too—wanting to feel his warm skin.

I bite back a moan as he dips his fingers into me.

"War," I whisper against his lips, "we can't do this here."

"I know, Sunshine," he whispers back. "I promise we will find some privacy where I can properly fuck you, but I cannot start my day without a taste."

He pulls his fingers from my wet pussy and brings them to his mouth, sucking them clean. I blush and then kiss him so that I can have a taste too. I don't know if it is the magic of bonding or the soul sharing or if it is just War, but I want him all of the time. I can't get enough.

"I love you," I say as I press my face into his neck, taking another moment of comfort before we need to start our day.

"I love you too, Ro," he replies softly as he squeezes me tightly.

After one final kiss, I climb off of War's lap and reach my hand out to help him up. I am stiff from sleeping in the same position all night. But I was honest with War when I told him that I only needed him. I have never felt safer than when I am in his arms. I just wish the Dreena drama wasn't happening.

"So, what's the plan, Stan?" I ask. He chuckles. I'm guessing that it didn't translate properly.

"The hunters returned late last night but I kept them separated from the females. We need to find out who all were involved, gather all of the information that we can before deciding on their sentence. Then, we are going to leave. The others will head out tomorrow with Zeke as a lead, but I refuse to stay here any longer than we have to. You deserve a bed and a bath and some proper food."

"What will their options be?"

"That depends a bit on who was involved. Neither of these couples are True Mates. They can be separated if they were not all involved in this scheme. I spoke to my brothers last night while you were sleeping. They will not allow Dreena into their packs. I doubt they would welcome these wolves into their packs for the same reason."

"But there is a pup," I remind him. I know that War would not blame the child for the actions of his parents, but I also know what it is like to suffer the consequences of your parents' mistakes. My parents decided to leave my sisters and I alone for days at a time so that they could get high. Ramsey's teacher had requested a wellness check after Ramsey did not show up to school for an extended time. The police officers found us unbathed, underfed, and alone. Ramsey was 8, I was 4, and Reese was only 2. We never saw our parents again.

"There is. And we will determine the best solution for him after we learn and weigh all of the facts. The females are sisters, and the males choose to live with the females as mates, but they have not given the commitment of a bonding ceremony and they are not True Mates."

Zeke joins us as we make our way over to their homes. The guards remain at the doors in their wolf forms. There are two men standing with them. They don't look angry. They look tired. Maybe even disappointed. If these are the hunters, I really don't think that they were involved in whatever is going on here.

War positions me at his side. Other than last night when we cautiously entered the village, knowing that something was off, he always has me stand next to him. I know that he does it as a show of power and respect. He wants the pack to see that he sees me as his equal, and therefore, they should too.

Holding my hand, he addresses the men. "Fiske, Sylas."

"Alpha," they both reply, lowering their heads in respect.

"Can you tell me what happened here last night?"

Both men raise their eyes to look at us. They keep their shoulders slumped and their voices calm. "We left for a hunt early yesterday morning," Fiske says. "The night before, we had received a message that you would be arriving. We wanted to hunt for some fresh game to offer you upon your arrival but were delayed by a storm."

"Our females told us that they would prepare the lodgings for your arrival," Sylas added, confusion clear in his eyes.

"Did you have any other visitors to the village recently?" War asked. Of course, we already know the answer to this.

"One wolf stayed here for a night on her way through. She said that she was traveling to visit family in Nighthowl. Our females knew her from when they were children. Dreena?" Sylas looks to Fiske to confirm the name. "We were not here for most of her visit. The game has been moving further away from the outpost, so we have been traveling farther to hunt."

"What is going on, Alpha?" Fiske asks. "When we returned last night, they would not let us enter our homes and we saw you sitting by the central fire. Did something happen?"

"Yes," War replies. "But I would like to talk to your females first."

Their doors are opened and the women come outside with the child. I am still very new to this world, and I do not know how the pack handles situations like this—but I overheard way more conversations than I should have growing up. I do not want that for this little boy.

"Heka," I keep my voice calm but firm, "can you please take this little guy to play with the other kids?" Heka nods and scoops up the young pup. She tickles him and says something about finding a treat.

"Zya. Zuri." War addresses the women by name. Instead of responding with the proper "Alpha" like their males did, they remain silent. I can see War's jaw tick.

"Zya," Fiske scolds. He clearly does not approve of her behavior. Her face turns red as she keeps her eyes down.

"Zuri, what is the meaning of this?" asks Sylas.

Zya remains quiet, looking down at the ground. She wrings her hands nervously. Zuri, on the other hand, raises her head to look me in the eyes and then spits at me. Before it even lands on me, War's wolf launches himself at Zuri, ripping through his clothing, knocking her to the ground and holding her neck with his teeth. Zeke stands by my side, ready to protect me if anyone else attacks.

Unable to remain quiet, I steel my spine. "Why?" I ask Zya. "Why would you do any of this? Who stole from the Alpha? What is the reason for such disrespect?"

Trembling, Zya looks at her male. Her eyes are full of regret. "I am sorry, Alpha. Dreena came to the village a few days before your arrival. She told us that our Alpha was put under a witch's spell. Black magic. She told us that you tricked him into mating so that you could siphon his power and destroy our pack." Zya starts to cry but continues, "She told us that if you were ever to stop here, you would siphon our magic too. I didn't want to believe her. But she said that she decided to leave the pack because you tried to steal her magic too—that if she didn't leave, she wouldn't have had any magic left to shift between forms. Zuri decided that we needed to make it so that you do not stay here."

"What happened to War's belongings? His lodging is empty."

"Dreena took what she could. She said that you stole everything from her, so she was only taking what was owed. Zuri burned the rest," Zya confesses quietly.

"War held me by the central fire all night so that I could rest after days of travel. He did that because he loves me. Not because I am a witch. Not because I have forced him to bond with me so that I can ruin the pack." I
157

slowly take off my leather harness and then my dress, leaving me completely bare for the pack to see. Zya, Fiske, and Sylas gasp. They didn't see our markings before because of the clothes we wore. "War and I are Mated because we are True Mates. Our souls pulled us together across worlds. During our bonding, we received these markings," I drag my finger across the tattoo, "We are Moon Touched."

I give them a minute for that to sink in. "I am not a witch. I came into this world without any magic in my veins. Any powers that I now have, were gained through bonding with my soulmate. Instead of trusting your Alpha to do what is best for the pack, you believed the words of a liar. Dreena was banished from the pack because she attacked me. She was jealous that War refused to take her to his bed and was behind several failed attempts to eliminate me before she tried to rip out my throat. War's wolf had sentenced her to death, but I convinced him to be lenient. I will not make that same mistake again." I take a moment to breathe. I do not hide my anger—or my hurt. They need to understand the grave mistake they have made.

"Dreena will die if she continues this crusade across the territories. The Alphas of Nighthowl and Nightfury will stand with their brother. I suggest you think about where your loyalties lie. Your sister will be punished for the disrespect she has shown today. But you chose to tell the truth. I do not believe that you are a threat to me or our pack, but it is War's wolf that will ultimately decide."

Zeke crosses over to where War has Zuri pinned to the ground. Once he has hold of her, War shifts and stands behind me, banding his arm around my waist.

"I am so sorry, Alpha," Zya says. "Fiske and Sylas did not know that we did not prepare your lodging. They did not know that Dreena had stolen from you or that she spoke such hateful lies. I regret listening to Dreena and my sister. I was only trying to protect my child."

"Thank you for your honesty. I agree with Rowan. I believe you were led astray. Those who spread hate are often the loudest." War says. Turning to Zuri, he continues, "You have shown great disrespect. I will not tolerate attacks against my Mate—be it physical assault or vicious lies. If you do not believe that my Mate and I are worthy of your respect as your Alpha, you do not belong in the Nightfang pack."

I keep my eyes trained on Zuri; my face is as neutral as I can manage. I know that, if he decides it is warranted, I will not step in to advocate for her life. Maybe that is callous of me—but I did so with Dreena and look at where that got us. This world is different from the one that I know. Maybe the harsher consequences are necessary.

"You have two choices," War continues. "You may leave my pack and try to join another. It is doubtful that they will accept you, knowing how easily your loyalty was tarnished. Your second option is to stay. You will need to apologize to my Mate. You will also need to replace everything of mine that was burned or stolen. And it will be *you* replacing those items—not your sister or your male. You will hunt the game and process the furs. You will sew the blankets and clothing. You will purchase the soaps and bath oils. You will do it all on your own. There will be a guard assigned to you to make sure that you follow through with this sentence."

Turning to Sylas, War says, "You live as mates but are not actually bound. If Zuri chooses to leave, you are welcome to stay. If you decide to leave, my brothers would accept you into their packs. If she stays, you, Zya, and Fiske will not lift a paw to help her serve her sentence."

Sylas, Fiske, and Zya all nod their understanding. War addresses Zuri again.

"You will make your decision now. Rowan and I have a long day of travel ahead of us since we do not have a place to stay in this village. If you choose to stay, Zeke will assign a guard to you, and you will replace my items within two moons. If you decide to leave, you will be escorted out of my territory within the hour."

Looking towards Zya and Sylas, Zuri makes her decision. "I choose to stay," she tells War. Then, turning to me, she apologizes. "I am sorry for the disrespect that I have shown you. I should not have trusted Dreena. I will work hard to atone for my mistakes."

Leaving the safety of War's arms, I step towards Zuri and take her hands in mine. "I am new to this world and its customs. But something that my sisters and I learned early in life is that hurt people, hurt people. Dreena used fear to manipulate you. You almost lost your life today because of it. In the future, please choose kindness."

Zuri nods her head and then takes a step back. I return to War's side, realizing that we are still both completely naked. Most of the crowd dissipates as the matter has been mostly resolved. War discusses some things with Zeke while Heka approaches me with our bag.

"I have packed some food for your journey today," she tells me.

"Thank you. Are you sure you don't want to return with us?"

"Oh, child. I am not as quick as I once was. Warrick will need to make good time without stopping if you wish to sleep in a bed tonight. I will travel with Zeke and the rest of our hunting pack. We will only be a day or two behind you."

Giving her a hug, I say goodbye. I quickly get dressed while War scarfs down some food. I will be able to eat along the way, but he does not plan to stop for himself. A few moments later, War shifts—his wolf ducking between my legs to scoop me up onto his back. He takes off at a sprint.

Since we are now traveling alone, I do not have the children to help pass the time. During the heat, War had told me that he thinks we will be able to communicate mind to mind, like he does with his brothers and his pack. Focusing, I look within myself to try and figure out my powers. I can still feel that sense of 'other' radiating in my chest. Not really sure what to do, I try to imagine it as a string connecting us—similar to the pull that we feel from our souls. When I follow the string, it feels like it goes under a locked door. After hours spent trying to force it open, I decide to take a break before I drive myself mad. *Knock, knock? Who's there? My sanity.* I snort.

"I will love you even if you lose your mind, Sunshine." I startle so suddenly that I almost fall. War has to slow down and shift his body while I frantically

grasp at his fur to stop myself from splatting on the forest floor.

"Were you…did I…Did it actually work? How did I do that?" I ask out loud.

"Our connection opened up. It could have been something that you did—or maybe it just needed a little longer to develop. How does your head feel? Any pain?" he says in my head.

"This is so strange. I have been trying all day to figure something out and just when I was ready to throw in the towel, there you were—clear as day in my head. This magic stuff should really come with an instruction manual."

"But does it cause you any pain?"

"I don't think so. I was starting to get a headache from doing mental gymnastics for hours straight—but I don't think that communicating is causing any pain."

"Try speaking to me with your mind again."

Oops. I forgot that I could do that. *"What would you like me to talk about?"* I ask with a smile on my face.

"Anything. I want to know everything about you."

"Well, my favorite color has always been blue—but now it is the exact icy blue of your eyes," I admit. *"When I was six, a boy at school pushed me down on the playground and told me that only boys were allowed to like*

blue and that I was never going to find a family to love me if I didn't act like a girl."

"What happened to the fuckwad?" he asked with a growl.

I giggle. *"Ramsey beat him up and then made him give me all of his fancy blue crayons and markers."*

I can hear War bark a laugh in my head and the wolf's chuff of laughter out loud.

"Ramsey always took care of Reese and me. We hadn't found a family by the time that she turned 18— that's when humans are considered adults in my world— so she legally became our guardian. She worked three jobs to support us while we finished school. I miss my sisters so much," I confess.

"If they are here, we will find them, love."

I nod and let the tears fall. I still have not fully processed my feelings about being separated from them. I have been telling myself that I will find them, but the truth is, we don't even know if they are in this world. They could be back in New York driving police officers crazy trying to find me. Or worse, they could have been captured by the traffickers too. I try not to let that thought take root. They are okay. They need to be okay.

Leaning down, I wrap my arms around the wolf's neck and nestle my face into his fur. He slows down his run just a little to keep me from jostling too much. Staying snuggled into his fur, I drift off into a light sleep.

A few hours later, War shifts—spinning and holding me tight to his body. He hugs me for a long while before tilting my chin up for a kiss.

"Are you ready to meet my brothers?" he asks.

I hadn't even realized where we were. Looking around, I see a city. It does not have skyscrapers and a non-stop flow of taxis cluttering the streets—but it is a city of lodgings spanning out as far as I can see. In the center, raised on a bit of a hill and surrounded by fields, is a castle-like lodge. This is War's home. We made it.

Chapter Thirteen

Rowan

War puts on some clothes and then walks with me hand in hand towards the center of the village. It takes us over an hour to make our way into the center. There is a large outdoor market area filled with open stands where vendors can sell their wares. There are also food stands and pub-style restaurants that I can't wait to try. We would have arrived much faster if we hadn't walked, but it felt nice to weave between streets and explore on foot. It is fully dark as we arrive outside the door. Everyone who we passed greeted War with respect. I received some curious looks, but nothing hostile.

The entire pack is aware that War has taken a Mate, but the details of our bonding have not been disclosed. Our Moon Touched markings are covered right now. War would like to make a formal announcement after I meet his family, and we are settled.

"Are your brothers both here already?" I ask as we walk through the grounds that surround the lodge.

"Bade and Griff should both be home. They knew that we would be arriving tonight, so they are probably still up."

"And your parents?" I realize he has never spoken of his parents. He has told me about his brothers in great length—maybe because I only ever talk about my sisters.

"My mother died when my brothers and I were pups. Complications of childbirth. My father is here somewhere, though I am not sure if he was made aware of our arrival. He turned into a bit of a ghost after losing his Mate."

I nod and wrap myself around his arm, giving him a squeeze.

Stepping closer, the large wooden door opens before us, and we are greeted by two women who must be employees of some sort. War did not mention his brothers being Mated, so I don't think that these women are here for a personal matter. War thanks them as they take our bag and we continue further into the house. Unlike the tents and temporary lodgings that we have been staying in—this castle-like lodge is a fully permanent structure made from wood and stone. There are walls separating rooms, polished stone floors, and stairwells. I don't want to get my hopes up, but if there is an actual toilet here, I might cry.

Entering a large but cozy living room, we stop before two large men who are standing in front of the fireplace. There is no doubt in my mind that these are War's brothers. Nearly identical in size, they both have the same ice blue eyes and bone structure that I know well.

One of the men has his chestnut-colored hair cut short. I wouldn't call his clothing fancy, but what he is wearing is definitely more formal than War's leather pants and cottony-feeling shirts. He looks like he would feel much more comfortable in a library than a battlefield. I would bet all of my non-existent money that this is Griffin.

The other man is possibly the most intimidating of the three. Bade stands just as tall as his brothers but has an unmatched bulk of muscles. His hair is almost the same blond as mine, shaved on the sides and braided down the middle. When I think of Vikings, this is what I picture.

Give him an axe and a longboat and he would look right at home invading and raiding coastal lands. He wears only a pair of leather pants, and I get the impression that Griffin made him put them on to greet us. The way that he looks at me makes me think that he is a little more wolf than man.

"Brothers, this is my Mate, Rowan," War introduces. "Ro, these are my brothers Griffin and Bade."

"It is really nice to meet you," I say.

Griff smiles and pulls me into a hug. "Welcome to the family. I have so many questions."

I laugh, "I have almost no answers." He chuckles in response and bats at War's hand as he tries to pull me away.

Bade gives me a nod in greeting but remains quiet. War told me ahead of time that Bade is a wolf of few words, so I don't take it personally.

"I'm sure that you would like to get some rest. We can get to know each other more in the morning," Griffin says. "Your quarters have been prepared. I put some clothing in your room that should work okay until the clothier is able to get your measurements. We haven't had a female living in the lodge since our mother was here, so the options were limited."

"Thank you," I say. "I have gotten used to wearing War's shirts, but it would be nice to have something that actually fits. In the world that I came from, humans are not allowed to be naked in public, so it has been a bit of a learning curve for me." In a quieter voice I ask, "Is underwear even a thing here? I have really only had this guy to ask and I'm not sure I trust his answer."

Griffin laughs. Bade lets out a quiet chuckle.

War wraps his arms around me from behind and not so quietly says in my ear, "I told you that undergarments will only get in the way. I like having unrestricted access to your pussy."

Both Griffin and Bade snort out laughs as my face turns bright red.

"Did you just refer to her cunt as a feline?" Bade asks. Griffin hits him and War growls.

"Yes," I answer for War, "but some things don't translate quite right. There are a lot of words that are used while talking about...uh...female anatomy. Vagina, pussy, cunt, cooch, vajayjay, girly bits, beaver, hoo-ha..."

"I think they get the idea," War says.

I shrug and give him an innocent look. "I'm just trying to be informative."

"And it is my favorite subject," War says, "but I would much rather have a front row seat during this lesson."

I giggle and turn in his arms. He seals his mouth to mine in a deep, passionate kiss. It has been far too long without his touch, and I press my body to his with a moan.

"And…that is our cue. Come on Bade. Let's let the lovebirds pretend to rest," Griffin says.

In this moment, I couldn't care less where we are or who is around. I am consumed by War's kiss as he picks me up and carries me to what I am assuming are his quarters. He doesn't stop moving until we pass into a room and he kicks the door closed behind us. Laying me down on the bed, he undoes the leather bindings on my harness while I rip at his pants with less finesse.

Our lips part only long enough for our shirts to be pulled off over our heads.

"I know you probably want a bath, some food, and a solid night's sleep—but I need to be inside you first," he says against my neck as he trails kisses down my body. I pant as he pulls my nipple into his mouth, flicking the bud and then biting down. My clit throbs, begging for the same attention.

"Fuck first," I say between moans. "Then bath. Then you can eat me and fuck me again. I can sleep while we are knotted."

"Fuck, you are perfect."

War enters me in one hard stroke. He kisses and bites at my skin, the pain only adding to the pleasure as he pounds into my pussy. An orgasm crashes through me as I scream his name.

"Reach down and squeeze my knot, Ro. I need to have you several times tonight so I'm not going to lock you yet."

I reach my hand between us, moaning when I feel how wide I am stretched to fit his massive cock. I squeeze him gently, pulsing my grip a few times before clamping down tight. He roars his release, filling me so full his cum splashes out onto my hand.

After catching his breath, War scoops me up and brings me into the bathroom. "Sweet baby Jesus," I say under my breath.

"What?" War asks as he looks around, unsure as to what I am freaking out about.

"Is that a toilet? Like an actual, real, properly working toilet?"

"Yes..."

"How are you not more excited by this? Oh…right…you have been here before and were not under the impression that you would need to find a bush anytime you needed to take a shit."

War laughs at me. "Do you need to use it now?"

"Not really, but I kind of want to just for old times' sake. You really have indoor plumbing, and you didn't think to tell me?"

"Wolves shit in the forest all of the time. I really did not think about it," he shrugs.

"Well, prior to coming here, I had only ever used toilets. Other than this one time when I chugged a giant Slurpee and I had to squat in an alley behind a dumpster because I couldn't wait until we got back home."

War tilts my chin, returning my focus to him. "I do not want to give you heart issues, but I feel like I should tell you that the water for the bath does not need to be warmed up and brought in with buckets. It just comes up through the pipes."

"I think I might need to sit down," I say—being mostly dramatic but a little bit serious.

War continues laughing as he fills the tub with hot water and adds in some delicious smelling oils and salts. "Why don't you come and sit with me in the bath? You can continue being amazed while I wash you."

War's bath is built into the floor and is much bigger than the tubs he had in his tents. I climb in with him and then cozy up next to him. With my back flush to his chest, I can feel his cock pressed against my ass.

"How are you hard again already?" I ask. "If you were human, you would need to seek medical attention at this point."

War chuckles. "I am in a constant state of arousal when I am with you. It is actually quite the problem considering I am a wolf some of the time."

I snort. "Just to be clear, I'm not complaining. I am just a little worried about your health."

He nips at my ear. "Try to relax while I wash your hair and shave you. You will not be getting much sleep tonight."

True to his word, War keeps me up most of the night. It is very early in the morning when I finally fall asleep, completely sated, and knotted, in the arms of my Mate.

Chapter Fourteen

War

I was only asleep for a few hours, but I feel happy and rested when I wake. Ro is still asleep next to me. Her hair is a wild mess of golden curls. Her lips are swollen and bruised from our lovemaking. Her breasts are covered in marks from where I nipped her—though they would all disappear soon with her advanced healing.

Gently skimming my fingers over her body, I trace them down her chest, past her hip, and over the perfect curve of her ass.

Finding her center still leaking from being filled has me needing a taste. I roll her to her front, careful not to wake her, and pull her towards the edge of the bed.

Placing a pillow under her abdomen, I settle her onto her knees. Her perfectly pink pussy and tiny asshole are right where I want them. Kneeling behind her, I slowly lick. She tastes amazing. Her sweetness was made salty by my release still inside of her. I could spend all day like this.

Rowan starts moaning in her sleep, making me smile against her skin. I press my thumb to her clit while slowly fucking two fingers inside of her. She moans again, making me chuckle. My Mate loves having my mouth on her. She begs for it even in her sleep. Dragging my tongue from her cunt up to her ass, I gently rim her tight hole. Rowan told me that she has never given this hole to another man and I desperately want to claim it for myself.

She is so tiny that she will need to be properly prepped before being able to take me. Continuing my ministrations, I let my tongue slip into her back hole while pumping my fingers in and out of her pussy.

I feel Rowan tighten and then relax again as she moans my name and pushes back towards me. "That's it, love. I know you are close. Go ahead and come on my fingers."

Within seconds, she does just that, moaning and convulsing as the waves of pleasure crash over her.

"Are you going to let me fuck this pretty hole?" I ask her as I bring my soaked fingers up and gently press one into her ass.

"Yes, please. I need you, War," she replies—her voice raspy with sleep.

"Let me get you ready first, okay? I want you to come on my fingers again while I stretch your ass."

"I want to taste you, War. Let me taste you while you stretch me." Her words are filled with desperate need.

Pulling away from her, she whimpers. I climb back onto the bed with her. Laying on my back, I flip her around so that she can reach my cock while I lick and stretch her. She immediately wraps her lips around the head of my cock, licking up the precum that had already started to leak. She moans around me as I pull her down to my face, rubbing her clit with my chin as I feast.

I work one glistening finger into her before adding a second. Spreading my fingers, I stretch her open before I add a third.

Squeezing my knot while she sucks hard on my cock makes me lose control. I thrust up into her mouth, hitting the back of her throat and making her gag twice before emptying myself into her.

"Drink every drop, Sunshine."

I widen my fingers in her ass and nip at her clit, causing her to flood my face with her release.

Gently removing my fingers, I flip us around and thrust my cock into her dripping pussy. She is still shaking and moaning when I ask, "Are you ready, love?"

She nods her head and says something into the pillow. I pull my cock from her cunt and begin to press it into her puckered hole. I go slow and steady as I fuck into her, pushing a little further each time until I am fully seated. Giving her a chance to adjust around me, I kiss down her spine and pinch her nipples. Rowan is panting and clawing at the bedding, but she pushes herself back towards me, encouraging me to move.

I have to concentrate on not coming immediately. She is so warm and tight. She is sweating, moaning, and mumbling things that I do not understand.

"You are doing so well, love," I praise. "You are taking every inch of my cock into your tight ass." Her muscles are pulsing around me and I know that she is close. "Go ahead and let go, Sunshine."

My words must be just enough because one thrust later, she shatters around me and I shoot my seed so deep within her, she will be dripping for days.

Pulling out of her, I lay down and drag her onto me. Rowan's cheeks are flushed glisten with sweat and tears. "Did I hurt you, Ro?"

Despite the tears, she gives me a dreamy smile. "You didn't hurt me, Big Guy. I have never felt so amazing."

I tuck a piece of hair behind her ear and kiss her forehead. Rowan falls back asleep as we lay there, tangled up together. I must doze off too because sometime later, I am awoken to the sound of someone entering my wing of the lodge.

Covering Rowan up with a blanket, I almost make it to the door when my father flings it open and brushes past me as he enters my room. My wolf growls, not wanting anyone near our Mate while she sleeps.

Blocking his view of my bed with my body, my father finally looks up. His eyes go wide at the sight of me. It is not my nakedness that he is shocked by but the Moon Touched markings across my chest.

"War?" I hear Rowan's voice call for me as she sleepily sits up in bed. Rushing over to her, I help wrap a blanket around her, giving her the modesty that I know she prefers. She gets up and peeks out from behind me.

"Ro," I say, "this is my father, Lycus. Father, this is my Mate, Rowan."

"Well, this is awkward," she says quietly. "I was hoping to meet you with a few more clothes and a little less...um...sticky," I snort, and she hits me before she continues, "but it is nice to meet you."

My father shakes himself free from his silent shock. "Uh...yes...well, I probably should not have barged my way in here. Your brothers did not tell me that you were not alone. Maybe we can try a different introduction over breakfast," he suggests, quickly turning and making a break for the door.

As soon as he is gone, Rowan doubles over laughing. I laugh with her as I throw her over my shoulder and carry her into the bath.

We are both quite hungry, not having eaten actual food last night so we quickly clean ourselves up and head out to find breakfast. Finding my brothers and father in the great room, I dish up two full plates of food before sitting down with Rowan at the table.

My father is looking at his food, avoiding eye contact with us while my brothers both have smirks.

"You assholes could have told Father that Rowan was here with me," I say.

"We thought you would want to share the good news yourself," Griff says with a make-believe air of innocence.

"Besides, I am not sure how the old man did not hear that you had company last night. And this morning," Bade adds.

"Oh god," Rowan says, covering her face with her hands.

"You do seem to like that phrase," Bade mumbles.

"Ignore him," I say, pulling Ro's hands from her face. "He is just jealous because his charming personality has not won him the same bedmate for more than one night."

Bade scoffs and Griff smirks.

Rowan's stomach grumbles so I lift some food to her mouth. She remains quiet, but continues eating.

"Anyway," I change the subject, "there are some things that we would like to discuss with all of you. First, I would like to hold a celebration in honor of our bonding. Not many have fully been made aware and I think it would be beneficial to show support throughout the packs."

"And if any of you can think of a way to stop the idea of me being a witch from spreading around, that would be peachy," Rowan adds.

"Why would they think that you are a witch?" my father asks.

"A former pack member became butt-hurt when War refused to reject me and sleep with her, so she attacked me," she explains.

"She actually tried a few times, but we did not find out the extent of her efforts until she confessed," I add.

Ro nods and continues, "I convinced War to banish instead of kill and now she is spreading lies about me to anyone who will listen," Ro explains. "Just for the record, I am not a witch. There isn't even any magic where I am from."

"We will figure it out," I say, squeezing Ro's hand.

"What changes have you noticed so far?" asks my father.

"I can heal much quicker," she says.

"When Ro first appeared before me, she was covered in bruises and cuts. She almost died from an infection, but Heka was able to save her." I pull out her shirt a little bit to sneak a peek at her chest. "It looks like bruises and bites can heal within a couple of hours now."

Rowan's cheeks flush so I give her a playful wink.

"We, um, can also speak mind to mind," she continues. "I haven't tried with anyone but War and most of the time I forget that I can even do it."

"Any headaches?" asks Griff.

"Not so far. And I can feel a sort of well of power in my chest, but I don't know what it is," she says.

Griff and Bade both look over at me. I have not discussed my theory about Ro's power with her yet.

"I have an idea, something that I noticed earlier this morning, but we need to move this discussion to the garden to see if I am right," I say.

We all stand and exit the lodge at the rear of the house. When my father was Alpha, he oversaw all three packs, just like his father before him, and the lodge was our family home—right in the center. My mother had a huge garden that she tended to. After she died, most of the garden died with her. Heka uses a small portion to grow special herbs for medicines and there is still a plot for vegetables, but the flowers have mostly all withered.

Even without the vibrancy that flowers bring, the garden is beautiful. Stone arches and benches dot the space. A stone path winds through the barren beds. In the center lies a sculpture of my mother's wolf with three pups playing at her feet.

Rowan walks over to the sculpture and places her hand on the wolf's head. "What was your mother's name?" she asks me softly.

"Helen," my father replies with a tear in his eye.

With one hand still on the sculpture, she kneels and places her other hand on her heart. Rowans closes her eyes and remains there for a long moment. When she opens her eyes, we all gasp. Flowered vines spring up out of the ground, growing up along the wolf's back and settling into a crown upon her head.

"What just happened?" Ro asks in shock.

"You," I reply.

"Me? How did I do that?"

"I think it is part of the power that you were blessed with," I explain. "I noticed it as we travelled here. The forest came to life all around us in a way it never has before. The temperature has been warmer. Flowers began to bloom even though there should still be a morning frost."

"Are you sure? I did that?"

"I believe so."

"But how? I didn't even know I was doing it. And this," she points to the flowering vines, "how did I do this?"

"What were you thinking about when you were kneeling?"

"I thanked her for bringing you into the world," she says quietly.

I wrap her in my arms. "And what were you thinking about as we ran through the forest?"

"A lot of things...but I guess mostly it all had to do with how beautiful it all was. And how, despite the circumstances that brought me here and the sadness that I feel for possibly never seeing my sisters again, how happy I am to be able to experience this world with you."

"Love," I say.

"Yeah?" she asks.

"No, love. I think that love is what triggered your power. Showing and experiencing love, even if not intentional, is what pulls your power out." I turn us around so that she can see the outdoor walls of the lodge on our wing of the house. "Look," I say, pointing.

Growing up along the stone are the same flowered vines that grew along the statue. The vines cover the walls in a dense weave of leaves and flowers, curling around the windows and balcony off of our bedroom.

"I did that? But when?... Oh god..." she covers her mouth with her hand.

"Maybe 'oh god' is the magic word," suggests Bade. Griff and my father hit the back of his head.

"That is not even the craziest part," I add.

"What could be crazier than me making plants grow with my magic pussy?" she whisper-shouts.

I snort. "While I do agree that your cunt is quite magical, I believe that it is what you feel while coming all over my fingers, tongue, or cock that makes the plants grow."

She stares at my mouth—her tongue peeking out to moisten her lips.

"Yeah, yeah. We get it—so much magical sex. What is the crazy part?" asks Griff.

"I checked in with Zeke this morning to see when they will be arriving today. They had to delay leaving because four females are sick. According to Heka, they are all pregnant."

"Okay...I'm assuming that often happens when a bonding ceremony turns into a fuck fest like ours did," Ro replies.

"Yes, sex can result in babies. But, for wolves, pregnancies do not happen very often anymore. It is actually a problem that we have been trying to find a solution to," Griff explains. "Four females falling pregnant in a single hunting party at the same time is unheard of. Were they all True Mate matches?"

"No. Only one pair are True Mates. They have two pups already," I explain.

"Eden?"

I nod. "These will be the first for the other three."

"But, that doesn't mean that I caused that. How could I make someone else pregnant?" she asks.

"We were not far from camp," I say. "I think that your power is related to fertility."

"I think I'm going to be sick," Ro mumbles. I help her sit down on a bench, holding her close as she wraps her head around all of this.

"If this is true, this is an amazing gift," Griff says. "I will need to do some research. I remember reading a passage from The Mother..." his thoughts trail off as I focus my attention back on Rowan.

"Are you okay, love?"

"No. I am actually going to be sick!" Rowan turns away from me and vomits all over the ground.

Chapter Fifteen

Heaving, I hear War and his brothers trying to figure out what is wrong.

"Poison?"

"Human illnesses?"

Valid options—though I know in my heart what it is. I haven't done a great job at keeping track of time while I have been here, but I think it has been about a month total—two weeks since our bonding.

"Stress?"

"Strain from using magic?"

I was on the pill back on Earth. I don't remember when my last period was, but I definitely haven't had one here unless it happened when I was nearly dying. I do not know anything, really, about heats other than that is when animals get all horny for each other. Prime breeding time, I guess.

"Research"

"Healer"

If women got pregnant just from being near me during my heat, what are the odds that I wasn't affected myself? Isn't it too soon to have symptoms? I should have paid more attention in Health class.

I heave again, though nothing is coming up at this point. War holds my hair and rubs my back.

If this is what I am pretty sure it is, we will have time to figure it out. Getting knocked up by my alien wolf shifter soulmate was not on my bingo card for the year, but I can pivot. Am I ready for this? No. But we will have time. Humans are pregnant for 9 months. That is plenty of time to figure this out.

More heaving.

Wait, humans have 9 months to prepare but how long do wolves have? Will that make a difference?

War and his brothers are still trying to figure out possible causes to my illness, but I make eye contact with Lycus. He gives me a soft smile and a little nod. He knows what this is too.

"War," my voice is quiet and raspy from puking my guts out. He keeps talking, still distracted.

Using my mind, I try again, *"War."* When he turns his attention back to me I ask, "How long are wolf shifters pregnant for?"

"Usually about 5 months," Griff answers as he looks up from a book. I didn't even realize he had left to find one.

"Do you... You think..." War stutters.

I nod.

War places his hand on my belly and looks into my eyes. His are glossy. He pulls my mouth to his and places a soft kiss on my lips.

I push him away. "I have puke breath," I tell him.

"I do not care," he replies, pulling me back in for another kiss.

After a slightly inappropriate make out session, given the audience, I pry myself from War and spin to sit on his lap. His large hand wraps about my body to hold my stomach.

"Hey Griffin," I say to get his attention back from his book. "Do you have any books on pregnancies between wolf shifters and other species? Human pregnancies last for 9 months, so I'm not sure what kind of timing to expect here."

"I will look," he says.

"And we will call in a midwife to confirm," says Lycus.

War stands and cradles me in his arms. "Bade, can you please put ears out for any possible threats related to Dreena feeling...what did Ro call it? Oh, 'butt-hurt.'" Bade snorts and nods, leaving the garden. "Griff, find whatever information you can in the books related to non-shifter and shifter pregnancies and Moon Touched powers relating to fertility." Griff nods and walks off while flipping through his book.

"I will speak to some of the staff about preparing for a celebration," says Lycus as he waves and walks away, leaving War and me alone.

"How are you feeling?" he asks.

"Good. Overwhelmed and nervous, but happy," I reply with a smile. "Are you okay with all of this? We didn't talk about any of this before we bonded," I ask timidly.

"More than," he replies with a kiss on my cheek. "In fact, I am so okay with it that I think we should go back to bed and have our own celebration," he says with a sexy growl.

"Is that right?" I kiss my way up his neck to his ear. "Are you going to make my magical pussy purr, Big Guy?" I nip at him.

He growls and sprints us into the house, taking the stairs two at a time. We spend the rest of the day celebrating—and purr I did.

The next few days go by pretty quickly. I spend a good amount of time with my face in the toilet—but when I am feeling okay, I work with Griff in the library trying to find any information that we can about my situation and what this all could possibly mean.

I have read through every book that Griff has about pregnancy. So far, it has all just been about wolf shifter pregnancies, but it is still helpful. We are going to just monitor my growth to try and come up with a due date. I really wish Ramsey was here.

War has been coordinating plans with the staff to prepare for a pack-wide party. It will happen next week so that it does not interfere with any full moon bonding ceremonies that may be taking place within the village.

Bade has been keeping track of any unrest that the packs may be experiencing as well as squashing any rumors that I am a witch.

From what we can tell, Dreena is still in Griff's territory. She has been able to stay one step ahead—but we can tell where she has been. She appears to be trying to build a pack of sympathizers, targeting small outposts and lone travelers. Unfortunately, it looks like she is having some success.

We have not told anyone other than Zeke and Heka about my powers—though the grounds around the lodge are nearly full of budding plants and the weather has been thrown into an early spring. I was worried that the change in weather could impact the environment negatively, but the change is slight enough that War doesn't think that it will be an issue.

The hunting party that we had been traveling with made it back to the village last night. Heka has looked me over and believes that everything is going well with my pregnancy. I would feel so much better if ultrasounds existed here, but Heka has been around for about 1000 years, so I trust that she knows what she is talking about.

A clothier just left after taking my measurements. I will need a dress for our party and some everyday clothing that I can wear, even when my stomach expands.

The clothing that is worn here is always functional and rarely covers much. Everyone is so used to shifting in and out of their wolf forms. The clothier and I discussed some skirt options made out of leather and the lighter material that War's shirts are made out of, as well as some bralette style tops. It all sounds pretty comfortable to me.

It has been an adjustment living in a place with staff members that come and go. Everyone has been friendly, but I know that they are curious about me. Some of the women stop talking when I enter the room, but I try not to think too much about it. My sisters and I would absolutely gossip a bit if the roles were reversed.

Speaking of my sisters, there has still been no word of them throughout the territories. I have no other option but to hope that they are here, safe, and that we will find them.

War and I eat our meals with Bade, Griffin, and Lycus. Heka too, if she is not busy with an appointment. It is a time that I have truly come to love. Seeing War with his brothers makes me miss my sisters, but I have also started to feel like part of the family and I couldn't be more grateful for their immediate acceptance of me.

The lodge quickly becomes my home, which is something I truly hadn't experienced before. Growing up, home always equaled people—my sisters. Here, it is both people and a place.

A week later, I am getting myself ready for our party when War sneaks up behind me and pulls my back flush against his body, placing a kiss on my shoulder.

"You look beautiful, love," he says. I am wearing an airy goddess style dress that shows off my moon markings. The material is almost see-through, but I am feeling more comfortable showing my body. I have my hair braided and twisted up off of my neck and am adorned with the cuffs from our mating ceremony.

"You are looking pretty good yourself, Big Guy," I say, turning in his arms to place a kiss on his lips. War is in his usual leather pants. He is without a shirt, putting his moon markings and his glorious muscles on display. I give his nipple a playful lick, causing him to growl.

I laugh and pull away to finish getting ready, but War grabs my arm to stop me. Walking the two steps back to him, he takes my face in his hands and kisses me. This kiss is sinful, full of pleasure and promise. He catches my moan with his mouth as he backs me up to our bed.

"We have a party to get to," I remind him, though I urge him to continue with my body.

"We have enough time," he says. "Besides, you are not quite ready yet."

"What do you mean?" I ask breathlessly.

Bringing his lips to my ear, he says, "We are not going out there until my cum is running down your legs." With that, he flips me over and rucks up my dress, exposing my bare pussy to him. He drops to his knees and has a taste.

"You are such a good girl—always so wet and ready for my cock," he says into my center.

Standing, he lines the head of his cock up and enters me in one long stroke. After giving me a moment to adjust, he fucks me hard and fast. He rubs my clit with his fingers as he pounds into me. I scream out my release, not caring that we have a house full of people who could probably hear. War fills me with his cum as my pussy spasms around him.

Slowing pulling out of me, he collects what has started to leak and pushes it back in with his fingers. Then, he tucks himself back into his pants, fixes my dress, and pulls me back towards the door.

Just like he promised, we entered the party with his cum leaking down my legs. I have been claimed by War—heart, body, and soul.

The party is starting with a feast. The lodge has been opened up for members of the pack to join us for a several course dinner. The doors leading from the lodge's large gathering room have been left open to the garden where more tables have been set up.

The party will continue all night, spilling into the streets of the village where there will be music and dancing.

All eyes follow us as we arrive at our table.

"Cutting it a little close, aren't we?" asks Griffin under his breath.

"Don't start," War says as we pass him.

"It seems you have already finished," mumbles Bade.

War and I laugh and take our seats. Before the food is served, War stands to give a toast.

"As many of you now know, a little while ago, I was fortunate enough to find my True Mate. Brought here from another world, our souls pulled us together. As you can see by our markings, we are Moon Touched. We recently found out that we are further blessed and our family will be growing. We are gathered here to celebrate love. We celebrate new life. We celebrate growth. We celebrate the good fortune that we share as a pack. There is still much unknown, but with my Mate by my side, we will thrive." Turning to me he says, "I love you, Ro."

"I love you too, Big Guy," I reply, blowing him a kiss.

Lycus stands and raises his glass towards me, "Welcome to the family." Shouts of cheers ring out throughout the lodge and the garden. The food is served, and the entire room breaks out into a flurry of different conversations. It is chaotic and wonderful. Despite the pack being so large, everyone seems to know everyone. It is so different from New York. Pack life is a really close community, and I feel lucky to be a part of it.

Throughout the night, I meet so many new people. Most of the women that I meet are so excited to hear about my pregnancy and disclose their own desires for pups.

Eden and the other pregnant females from the hunting party greet me with hugs. They thank me for sharing my magic with them. It is all still so strange to me, but they are all excited, so I am truly happy for them.

I make my way over to Heka. "Heka, is there any kind of contraceptive here?" I clearly did not think about this for myself.

"Yes, child. There is a tea that I can make and offer to those who do not wish to carry a child."

"Okay. Can we make sure to have that option known and available for everyone? I never want to take someone's choice away from them, especially when it comes to something as serious as pregnancy."

I really need to figure out a way to control my power so that I am not accidentally knocking people up.

"I will make sure that everyone knows about the tea, though I do not think many will want to take it. Most females that are of age want to have pups and have great difficulty falling pregnant."

Before learning about my magic, I didn't realize how big of an issue the pack was having with infertility. There were a few pups that traveled with the hunting party when I was found. I didn't realize that so few pups existed within the pack as a whole.

From what I now understand, wolves are most compatible with their True Mates. With a decrease in wolves finding their Mates, less pups are being born. Less pups being born lowers the chance of a True Mate being born—therefore continuing the cycle. It would be amazing if I could use my power to help.

I excuse myself from Heka and catch back up with War. He is making the rounds, meeting with as many pack members as possible. It is amazing to me that he is able to greet everyone by name. It is such a difference from my life in New York where I knew the name of one neighbor and the owner of the local bodega.

As the night grows darker, the party gets turned up a notch. Partygoers move through the streets of the village, drinking and dancing. Families have put their pups to bed and have returned to celebrate in various states of undress.

Lycus and Heka retired for the evening when the kids were also sent off to bed. I assume that Griffin and Bade have gone to find some company for the evening.

I am about ten seconds away from asking War to bring me to bed when he pulls me away from the crowd and pushes me up against the wall of a building. He covers my body with his own as he boxes me in. Grabbing both of my hands with one of his, he raises my hands above my head, holding me still. His other hand softly runs down the length of my arms, over my breasts, and down to my core. I can't help the moans that slip out. He is teasing me. Winding me up.

There is nothing gentle about the way that he claims my mouth. His tongue is hard and demanding, pushing into my mouth and stealing my breath. His mouth released mine only to continue on my neck. He nips and sucks along my collarbone, leaving marks as he goes.

"More," I beg.

I need his hands all over me. I press my hips forward, needing relief. War moves his hand away from my wrists—but I still can't move them. Looking up, I see why. Vines had grown up along the wall around us. They have wound their way around my wrists in gentle restraints.

"Clever girl," War chuckles. He rewards me by trailing his fingers up my thighs. So close to where I need him.

"Please, War," I whimper.

"Does my needy Mate want my fingers," he brushes his knuckles against my clit, "my tongue," he flicks his tongue over my pebbled nipple, "or my cock?" he grinds his hips against my body.

"I want it all," I moan.

"You want me to fuck you in the street where anyone could see?" he asks.

The risk of being caught sends a bolt of desire coursing through my body. "Yes," I whisper.

War growls as he lifts me up by my thighs. He pulls at the neckline of my dress, freeing my breasts. Leaning down, he sucks my nipple into his mouth. He continues pulling and teasing my breasts with his mouth, leaving bites behind as he moves from one side to the other. Reaching between us, he frees his cock but fills me with his fingers first—making sure that I am ready. I am soaked.

"I'm going to have to spank you when we get back to our room if you want me to fuck you out in the open." I can feel my pussy walls flutter against his fingers. He moans in response and impales me on his cock. The stone wall scrapes at my back as he ruts into me. The carnal display all around us mixed with the fast and dirty way that he is taking me against the building makes me shatter.

"Fuck," he groans. Ripping the vines away from my wrists, he pulls my dress back up to cover my breasts. War's wolf tears through his clothes, scoops me up onto his back, and takes off towards the lodge.

Concerned with this sudden shift, I ask, "What's wrong?"

"I need to knot you and I cannot do it here," he *explains.*

I laugh as we fly through the village. I don't think that the wolf has ever run this fast with me on his back before. In no time, we made it back to the lodge. The wolf leaps up the stairs, missing most of them as he goes.

There isn't anyone around, so I begin taking my dress off once we reach the hallway of our wing.

I land on our bed a moment later as the wolf dives between my legs, shifting back into War just as his tongue meets my center.

Though he was desperate to get me back to the comfort of our room to knot me, War takes his time. He whispers filthy and loving promises into my mind, adding to the pleasure. Our climax builds so slowly and powerfully that we can feel it in our souls.

Laying snuggled up with my Mate, still knotted, I am overcome by how much love I feel for this man.

"So…how many people do you think I got pregnant tonight?" I joke.

War throws his head back and laughs. Then, he peppers me with gentle kisses and caresses as I fall into a deep sleep.

Chapter Sixteen

Rowan

Every morning, War and I race to see who can wake the other first with our mouths. I swear War chooses to not sleep just so that he can win. Honestly, we both win regardless.

We then have breakfast with Lycus, Bade, and Griffin. Usually, Griffin has his face in a book and Bade discusses the ongoing Dreena problems with War and Lycus.

I found out that Lycus was once Alpha to all three packs. He has a twin brother who was his Beta. While it used to be common, War and his brothers are the last multiples to have been born alive. That was over 100 years ago. Heka told me that there have been some pregnancies of multiples since then, but they all resulted in loss of life for the babies, mothers, or both. War's mother died during childbirth with twins. The pups did not survive either.

After Helen's death, Lycus lost the will to lead the packs. His brother kept things under control until he was tragically killed in a skirmish with rogue bear shifters. That is when War, Bade, and Griff took over at the age of 17.

I spend every afternoon in the garden, trying to gain control over my power. I have figured out how to intentionally make plants grow. But those plants do not stay healthy unless additional doses of magic are poured into them. It makes me worried because I do not want the pregnancies that I caused to fail.

However, the plants that I grew unintentionally are strong and vibrant. They have even multiplied without my help. Flowering vines now cover the sides of the lodge. The weather has stayed pleasant, making it feel like spring even though we are still supposed to be in the cooler season.

Heka has all pregnant females come in for regular checkups so that we can monitor not only the pregnancies that have resulted from my magic, but also those who have occurred without my magical aid.

There have been several more pregnancies throughout the packs, but we have also seen losses.

"I was at the clinic today when Heka was called out for another loss. The mother survived but both babies passed." I am relaxing against War's chest in the bath after another long day. My eyes fill with tears as I think about that poor woman. "She was due in only another month."

War kisses my shoulder.

"I wish that I could gain more control over my power. I feel like I am making progress but then something happens, like today, and I know that it is not enough."

War turns my head so that he can look into my eyes. "While it is tragic—and it really, really is, Sunshine—you are not responsible for the loss that happened today. This is an issue that has been occurring within the pack for my entire life. I know that you were blessed with your Moon Touched magic to help the packs, but it is not solely your weight to carry. We will figure it out together."

He is right. Of course he is. But there is still so much that we do not understand about my power. Griffin has been pouring over his texts about Moon Touched pairings. From what he has found so far, those blessed by The Moon received great power—but no set examples were given. There are only a few Moon Touched pairings that have been recorded, and most of what has been written are stories from others who encountered them.

I capture his lips with mine, pulling him into a slow kiss.

"Have there been any updates on Dreena?"

War growls. He doesn't like it when I bring up her name, and I try to not ask too often, but I need to know. There is a fine line between stressing over what is happening and stressing over not knowing. War, Griffin, and Bade all have wolves keeping an eye on the unrest that has been increasing due to Dreena's efforts. There are now bands of wolves throughout the territories who believe our pairing to be unnatural. They believe the claim that I am a witch.

"Dreena has not attempted entry into the city, but she has convinced some outposts to join her crusade. I wish that I could silence her once and for all, but she has been able to evade our wolves who are tracking her. From what I know about her, she is resourceful but not overly powerful. She most likely has help."

"Is she still targeting small, secluded outposts?" Dreena has been smart as she rallies support. She quietly travels, only stopping at outposts like the one with Zya and Zuri.

"Yes. Not everyone follows her, but she has enough support now that it is making it difficult to manage communications throughout the packs. We cannot send out mass messages because she has wolves on her side who have not yet been released from the pack."

"Is she still in Griff's territory?"

"The last I heard. But she is working her way towards Bade's."

From what I understand, Bade's territory is sparsely populated, but his wolves are incredibly loyal. His outposts are run more like military bases. If Dreena does move into his territory, there is space for her to set up her own camp, but she will not gain any support. She will need to transport her own supplies versus taking over something that is already established.

"I do not think that Dreena will go into Nightfury until she has gained enough support," War adds.

"If I am able to gain better control over my magic, do you think that people will even want me to use my power on them? Rumors are already spreading like wildfire. I don't want to add more fuel to the flame."

The thing is, I can't even blame them for being wary of me. I appeared out of nowhere—from a completely different time and place. War and I immediately attached ourselves together. We know that it is because of our bond. And most that meet us also understand that our True Mate, Moon Touched bond is what brought us together. But, from the outside it could totally look like I have him under a spell. The great big Alpha who refused to settle down, took one look at me and never looked back.

Me.

The small human who has no wolf.

The small human who now has a great amount of magic.

Even wolves who do not believe Dreena's claim that I will be the end of the packs, still believe that I could be a witch. I have been approached by several females at the lodge and in the village who are wanting tonics or potions to be made to help increase fertility.

Heka has some teas that can aid in better reproductive health, so I just send them her way. I tried explaining that my magic does not work like that, but truthfully, I don't even know how it works.

False hope is something that I want to avoid. And, without a full understanding of what my magic can do, it is too risky. Sustaining pregnancy is just as difficult as becoming pregnant for the wolves.

"I think that there will be many who are eager to try. But we need to figure out what can be done first. You have been falling asleep during dinner most nights. I do not want you to push yourself too hard. You need to remember that you are growing life within yourself as well."

He puts his giant hand over my slightly rounded belly.

"Heka believes that there is more than one bun cooking in my oven." He chuckles but I can feel him tense. We both know the increased risk that comes with multiples. "There are a lot of things that I have come to love about this world, but the lack of ultrasound machines is not one of them. If we were back there, we would be able to see how many babies there are and what gender they are. We could hear heartbeats and take measurements to see how big they are growing."

"That does sound useful—though the doctor would be in for quite the shock if the babies are in their wolf forms when they check on them."

I giggle, placing my hand over his.

"Soon, my wolf and I should be able to hear any heartbeats fluttering around in there."

"Really? Is that how midwives are able to tell how many babies there are?"

"Yes, though mothers need to be further along before the midwives can hear it. I have extra sensitive hearing. It is something that might have been passed to you. Have you noticed it?"

"Now that you mention it, your snoring has become almost unbearable," I joke.

War throws his head back in a hearty laugh. "Is that so?"

A few days later, I am out working in the garden when I have a breakthrough. *"Come quick!"*

Mere moments later, War's wolf barrels through the door and skids to a stop right next to me. Shifting, he holds my face and growing belly in his hands. "What's wrong? Are you okay?"

I chuckle, "I'm fine. I'm sorry that I worried you. But I think I figured it out!" I exclaim.

Relieved to see that I'm not in any danger, War sits down.

"As you know, I have been trying to figure out why plants that I intentionally grow need additional boosts of magic while those that are grown unintentionally thrive on their own. To grow a plant, I have been pouring love into the seed, encouraging it to take root and reach towards the sky. Well, it is actually a little more complicated than that. Like with our connection, I started by visualizing strings but that morphed into more of a root system coming out of me, like a tree, and the roots lead to whatever it is that I want to grow. Then my magic flows through my roots, supplying power to what I am focusing on. Does that make sense?"

"I think so..."

"Good! So, you know how I helped maintain community gardens back in New York? When I first started volunteering, there was an elderly man named Joe who kind of took me under his wing. He taught me the basics of gardening. And when I was sitting here, I remembered something that he told me. He said, 'A garden can survive on sunlight and water, but for it to thrive it needs proper nutrition.' The nutrients are in the soil! I need to focus on the soil, not the plant itself."

I bring him over to an untouched garden bed to show him. I hold one hand to the earth and one to my heart. I can feel the power transferring from my chest to the soil as I pour love and health into the ground. The plants that begin to sprout do not immediately flower, but I know that they will with a little time.

"I can easily grow blooms to last a day, but by putting my magic into the soil, I can create an environment for the plants to thrive."

War picks me up and spins me around. "I'm so proud of you, Sunshine."

"I think that this is what I can do to help females who are having trouble falling pregnant. I can focus my magic on their womb, creating a healthy environment for the baby to grow."

"You are amazing," he replies, kissing me. "Show me again!"

Chapter Seventeen

Rowan

After another week of working with my power, I am feeling confident. The only issue is that in order to see if this is something that can help the females who wish to become pregnant, I will need to try with an actual person.

At breakfast, I update War's family about my progress. They have all seen my hard work out in the garden, but only War knows what I have figured out.

"Is it safe?" Lycus asks.

"I would not change anything about the female other than making sure that her uterus is healthy enough to support a pregnancy. Basically, I would ensure an ideal environment for a pregnancy to take hold. Obviously, I have not tested this on anyone, but the pregnancies that occurred as a result of our mating ceremony are all extremely healthy so far," War squeezes my hand, "Including my own. This morning, War was able to hear at least two different heartbeats separate from mine."

While we feel incredibly blessed, we all know that multiples have not been successfully born in over 100 years. Everyone gets up to give me hugs. I can see a flicker of worry in Lycus's eyes before he pulls me into a hug and offers his congratulations.

My babies feel a steady flow of love through my magic. I have to believe that it will all be okay.

"I have arranged for some females to come to the lodge for health assessments," Heka explains. There have been three failed pregnancies between the packs in the last couple of weeks. "Some of the females are currently pregnant and I want to keep a close eye on them. The others are females who have not had any success becoming pregnant. I planned to offer them some teas and tonics made from the herbs that you have helped me grow. Maybe you can accompany me to the appointments and see if there is anyone who would be interested in trying a direct dose of your magic."

"Eden is having lunch with me this afternoon. If she is okay with it, War will listen to see if she has multiples as well. She told me that this pregnancy feels different from her others.”

“We need to make sure to keep this quiet, at least for now,” Bade says. “Dreena’s support has spread in the wilds, but she does not have any real support within the village.”

“Heka, is there anyone that you can think of that we can trust with this? Ro’s safety is my top priority,” War says.

Heka hums. “Maha. Maha and Dune have been trying for a baby for over thirty years without any success. They are very loyal. Maha often helps out with births as well, so she has a full understanding of what has been occurring with expectant mothers.”

War nods. “Dune is out on a hunt right now, but I can call him back in so that he is here with her. He could be back by tomorrow.”

“Will it matter that they are not True Mates?” asks Griffin.

“I’m not sure. But not all who became pregnant due to my accidental influence were True Mate pairings. We need to make sure that Maha understands that we do not know what the final outcome will be. It is possible that it won’t work at all or there is still a chance of a miscarriage.

I do not have the ability to heal. I can only try to set them up for success."

Everyone voices their agreement and then we come up with a game plan for our next steps. Bade will continue to monitor the unrest and dispatch his pack when needed. Griffin will focus less on fertility in his searches and more on causes for failed pregnancies in wolves. War and I will meet with Eden and then I will accompany Heka to as many appointments as I can. Even if I cannot help everyone, I still want to learn more about pregnancy and childbirth. I can also help grow more medicinal plants for Heka to administer.

I grab War's hand and lead him out of the room. "Where are we going?" he asks.

"I need your help with something."

Over the last several weeks, I have been exploring the lodge. While having a clean break from my trashy reality tv obsession is probably for the better, there are moments during the day and night when I need something to silence my brain. When War is around, it is easy to be distracted from my anxiety. But, when he is gone—meeting with pack members or letting his wolf run—I begin to wander. Earlier this week, I found a hidden door.

Walking up to the bookcase that hides the door, War chuckles. Pulling on the lever hidden by a book about exotic plants, the door swings open for us.

"I see you found one of my mother's secrets," he says.

"I'm glad that I did," I reply. "When I found this room, I was unsure if anyone had been in here in a while. Is it okay for us to be here?"

War smiles. "Of course, love. You are welcome to any part of the lodge. Bade, Griff, and I found this room when we were boys. It was our mother's little hideaway. I have not been up here in a long time."

Skylights let sunlight in from above while colored glass covers the windows. When I first came here, there were pots with soil scattered throughout the room, but all of the plants were gone. I used some of my magic and now they are filled with life. Flowers and vines weave in and out of bookshelves and knickknacks. There is an incredibly comfortable leather sofa. I brought some furs and blankets up yesterday to make it even cozier.

War sits down, arranging me onto his lap so that I am tucked against him without putting any pressure on my growing belly.

"I accidentally took a nap here the other day," I confess. "It actually reminds me of our tiny apartment back in New York."

"Do you miss it?"

I think for a while—wanting to get my words right. "There are things that I miss about my old life—but I never really felt like I belonged there. I always felt out of place. I thought that it was because of how I grew up— moving from one temporary family to another—but now I wonder if it was because I was always meant to be here."

War pulls me into a languid kiss.

"I do miss my sisters though. I hope that they are okay."

"Even though we have not found them yet, it does not mean that they are not here. Our territories are vast, and with pack communication being limited, it might take us a little longer before we can find them. But we will, Sunshine. We will find them."

I nod and then we sit in comfortable silence, snuggled together.

"I am nervous to have these babies," I admit. "I am incredibly happy, and I love them so much already, but I don't know how to be a mom. Ramsey was the closest thing that I had to one. It is scary to do all of this without them."

War places his hand over mine and holds it to my bump. "You are going to be an incredible mother, Ro. I have seen how you interact with the pups—how you protected Zya's child while we dealt with that situation. You care deeply about others and are patient and kind. I am proud to be able to stand by your side every day and I am so fortunate to be able to raise these children with you. I love you, Sunshine. And I love our babies too. We will do this together, okay?"

I nod with tears in my eyes. Overwhelmed by the love that we share. "I feel guilty too." War turns my face, forcing me to meet his gaze. It feels important to say this all out loud, so I keep going. "I feel guilty because early on, I decided that even if I was able to find a way back to my world, I would never ask you to give up the life that you have here. It wouldn't be fair to you. So, I knew that I would stay. But now that we are having a family of our own, I feel guilty that I so easily gave up on returning to my sisters. That they might be back in New York, terrified that something terrible has happened to me. I feel guilty that, even if they are in this world, I am not able to devote all of my time to finding them. They might be in *this* world, scared and alone, or terrified. I was lucky that we found each other right away. But they could be anywhere. I feel guilty that we are so happy."

War brushes the tears from my face before bringing his lips to mine again in a gentle kiss.

"I might not have met them yet, but I know that your sisters would want you to be happy," he tells me against my lips. "It is okay to feel both happy and sad. It is okay to miss your sisters—to want them here—but to also be happy that you get to live your life here, with me and our children."

I feel raw, vulnerable, but safe. I know that every part of me is safe with War—even my truths. Needing more than his sweet kisses, I start tugging on his shirt. "I need you, Big Guy."

War pulls his shirt over his head and then brings his lips back to me, reassuring me of his love and support with each kiss. Working slowly, he rids me of my clothes, lowering his mouth to my peaked nipples, and working me into a needy frenzy.

"What do you need, Sunshine? You already possess all of me."

Working his cock free, I impale myself on it. I am ridiculously wet as I slide down his length, taking all of him into me.

Flipping our positions so that I am laying down on the sofa with him over me, our mouths crash together in a searing kiss. He lifts my leg as he thrusts into me, impossibly deeper. Slowly, but firmly, building our release. War makes love to me. And as my orgasm crashes through me, he locks us together, promising forever.

We lay together after and I doze on and off as I rest against his chest.

"Oh my god!" I exclaim—interrupting the calm.

"What is it?"

"I think I just felt the babies move." It was a small flutter. I almost missed it. But then it happened again. We both put our hands on my stomach but the movements are still too small to be felt from the outside. These babies are growing so much faster than they would if they were human babies.

Lowering his ear to my belly, War listens to their heartbeats. "I think that there are three."

Chapter Eighteen

Rowan

"It is so good to see you!" Eden rushes towards me as I finish putting trays of food on the garden table. "It has been a long time since I last saw this garden looking so colorful."

I give her a hug. "How are you feeling?" I ask her.

"I feel great. How are you doing?" She looks me over and notices my bump. "It looks like you are progressing like the rest of us."

"Yeah. We aren't really sure if this pregnancy will be the length of a wolf's or a human's—but I am definitely growing quickly." I look around the garden to make sure that we are alone. "War thinks that there are triplets," I say quietly.

Eden's eyes go wide but then quickly offers a smile.

"I have a few things that I want to share with you— but we cannot have the news spread." War and I discussed how much I could tell Eden, but decided that she can be trusted. Eden is my closest friend here. She has been through two successful pregnancies already and is Mated to her True Mate. I need to be able to talk to someone who isn't my Mate or his family—not that I can't talk to them, but I will need a woman's perspective on some things.

Eden nods her understanding. We sit down and start filling our plates to enjoy lunch while we chat.

"As you know, I have been blessed with some extra abilities since our mating. I have been working on gaining control and intention over my power, and I have had success. I haven't tried it out on anyone yet, but all of the plants that you can see around us are the product of my lessons."

"That is amazing Rowan. Do you think that this will be the answer to our problems?"

"Not fully. But I think that it can help. I am hopeful that by using my magic to encourage a healthy pregnancy, we will not see as many losses. But I don't have the power to intervene if something goes wrong. I have tried to help bring withered plants back to life without any success. I think that stretches past the scope of my abilities. I really wish that I could help save the lives of those lost during childbirth. One of my greatest fears is that I will help women become pregnant, but then their lives will be lost anyway."

Am I putting women's lives in danger?

Is it worth the risk?

I have to believe that it is. I have to believe that I was blessed with these powers so that I can help.

Eden reaches over and takes my hand in hers.

"You cannot carry that burden alone. I know that our pregnancies were not necessarily intended," she looks down at her growing belly, "but they *are* a blessing. Every time that my Mate and I come together, we know that it could result in a life created. My two children are proof that successful births can happen on their own."

That is true. Like Heka told me, there are contraceptive teas available for any that want it—but most wolves that are of age *want* to become pregnant. Most have been actively trying to become pregnant for years.

"Speaking of your children," I say with a smile, "does this pregnancy feel any different from your previous ones? We want to keep a close eye on our progressions."

"Honestly, my body feels great. I was so sick and tired with my others, but I feel healthy this time around."

"Would you be okay with War checking for heartbeats? With his advanced hearing, he is able to detect things earlier than the midwives."

Placing her hand over her stomach, she looks at me with understanding. "Do you think that it is multiples?" she asks.

"We think that there could be a good chance," I reply. "From what I have learned, multiples were the norm before the infertility issues began."

"Yes," she says quietly. "I need to know."

I nod my understanding. For the last 100 years, multiples have been a death sentence. Knowing what we are working with earlier on could help prepare for any outcome.

"We will figure this all out. But, one step at a time. Okay?"

Eden nods. Reaching out through our bond, I ask War to join us.

"Hey Big Guy, we are ready for you. Eden is nervous."

"I will call Arlo to join us as well," he replies.

"War and Arlo will be here soon," I tell her as I reach for another pastry. "What have the kiddos been up to? I would love for them to come by for a visit. I miss playing with them."

Eden jumps into a story about Madoc and Clover trying to make her breakfast the other morning as a surprise, which resulted in the entire kitchen and both pups becoming covered in flour. "We had to run them out to the river to bathe them in their wolf forms. I think we will be finding flour for weeks to come," she says with a laugh.

I giggle with her. I might not know much about being a parent, but I am truly excited for the level of chaos that kids bring to the table. War and Arlo walk into the garden a few minutes later. War greets me with a kiss while Arlo does the same to Eden.

"Are you sure that you want this?" I ask Eden, looking also to Arlo. Arlo whispers something in Eden's ear before she takes a deep breath and steels her spine.

They both nod. "We need to know so that we can be prepared."

"I will need to touch my ear to your stomach," War explains.

"Of course," Eden replies. She is wearing a loose tank top which she pulls up to expose her stomach. War kneels in front of her and brings his ear to her belly button.

The garden is silent. It is as if time itself has stalled while we wait for the news.

War pulls away and stands beside me but holds Eden's hand. "I hear two heartbeats," he says. "They both sound strong."

Eden gasps and then turns to face her Mate. A tear runs down her cheeks and he reaches out to wipe it away. Arlo takes her face in his hands.

"Breathe, my love," he says, kissing her forehead.

I am gutted by the fear that I know she feels at this moment. When she steps away from Arlo, I pull her into a hug. "There is much that we do not know about being Moon Touched," I say quietly to her, "but we do know that moon gifts are always positive. I have to believe that this is a good thing."

"Please know that you have our full support," War says to Eden and Arlo. "Heka will be your midwife, as long as you are comfortable with that."

"Of course," Eden replies. "She is the best."

"And, once it gets closer to delivery, you are welcome to move to the lodge with your family. That way, you will not need to wait for aid when labor begins."

"Ask Rowan about the flour incident and see if that offer still stands," she chuckles. "Clover and Madoc are a handful."

War places his hand on my belly. "We will welcome the practice."

"Thank you, Alpha," Arlo says.

After Eden and Alro leave, War walks with me back to our room.

"We will need to check the others," I say.

"I will talk to Heka about calling them in for appointments. We cannot share everything with them, but we can see if they would like me to listen. The more prepared we can all be, the better."

The next week flies by. The other three women who fell pregnant at our bonding ceremony came in for appointments. They all agreed to have War listen for heartbeats. All three women are expecting twins. This news is both terrifying and amazing. We need to make sure that everyone stays healthy throughout the pregnancies and survives the births—but it also means that my magic is helping to restore the natural order in wolf fertility. Multiples were a given before the issues began. Multiples will help to bring more life into the world quicker—which should allow for True Mate pairings to be formed again.

In addition to the expectant mothers coming in for appointments, Heka and I also met with Maha and Dune. When I explained what I wanted to do, they were willing to try. I made sure that they understood that all of the pregnancies that I know my magic helped create have resulted in multiples, including my own triplets. They have been trying to have a baby for so long, they felt the reward far outweighed the risk.

Heka has tracked Maha's cycle and believes that her heat will begin tomorrow. She has been coming to the lodge nightly for a dose of my power for the last couple of days. I have been pushing love and health into her with my magic. When her heat starts, her uterus should be an ideal environment for a baby to take root.

Heka has also been teaching me to become a midwife. I know that my power will not help if there is an issue during childbirth—but I want to be able to help in any way that I can. Even if that is just bringing fresh towels and being an encouraging hand to hold during delivery.

It is also helping to prepare me for my own delivery. Prior to all of this, my knowledge of labor and delivery came from binge watching Grey's Anatomy at 2:00am. If you would have told me a year ago that I would be pushing three babies out of my hoo-ha without any medication in the near future, I would have thought you were insane.

But it is going to happen. And we are all going to be okay. I am staying positive, learning what I can, and hoping for the best.

Heka, the midwives, and I have been doing home visits with some of the pregnant females throughout the packs. It has been nice to get out of the lodge and meet more people. Pack Nightfury actually has the most pregnant females in the village right now. When I asked Heka why that is, she explained that Bade only has soldiers at his outposts. All families and bonded pairs within Nightfury live in the village, whereas in Nightfang and Nighthowl, the outposts are often home to families.

In total, we have 36 pregnancies at the moment. We have been called out to help in two births this last week. Of the two, both were single babies born. One survived, one did not. Both mothers lived, though the mother who lost her child suffered from extreme bleeding. Heka explained that while wolves have accelerated healing, if the bleeding is bad, the healing cannot happen quick enough—especially when the mother's body is fighting to heal the baby as well.

I am heartbroken for the mother and the loss that she suffered. I feel responsible, even though this is a mother who conceived without my magic. I want to be able to fix this. We need to find a solution.

Chapter Nineteen

Walking into our quarters, I can hear Rowan's sobs. I was out with a small hunting party for most of the day today, but I know that there was a loss within Bade's pack. Rushing into the bathroom, I find Rowan in the tub. Her eyes are puffy, and her face is wet with tears.

I quickly climb into the water and pull her into my arms.

We stay like that until the water gets cold. I drain the tub and refill it with hot water, adding some soothing oils.

"Do you want to talk about it?" I ask. Ro takes a deep breath. I hold her to my chest as she starts to speak.

"Heka was called out to a birth in Nightfury. Eden and I were with her and decided to go and help since Maha's heat had started. The wolf that came to get us told us that there was bleeding. We grabbed all of the supplies that we could and rushed to the mother."

I can feel Rowan's body start to shake as she tells me what happened.

"We ran to her and were there within minutes. But the baby was already being born. Eden rushed in and caught the baby before he landed on the floor. Heka and I focused on the mother. There was so much blood. Too much blood. Heka helped deliver the placenta and then tried to slow the bleeding." Rowan turns to bury her face in my neck. I rub her back as she tries to breathe through sobs. "I poured my magic into her. I sent health and love into her—so much that I almost passed out."

An uncontrolled growl escapes my chest. I do not like the thought of her putting herself in danger.

"I am okay," she reassures me. "I used more power than I ever have before, but I didn't feel any of it take hold. It left my body but didn't do anything to help the mother. I now know for certain that my magic cannot heal." She sounds so defeated. I know that she was hoping that she could use her power to heal. "I couldn't do it. I wasn't enough."

"Ro, please do not think that, love. You are more than enough. You are everything."

She gives me a sad smile. "I just want to be able to help but mothers are still fighting for their lives and babies are still dying. I know that I didn't cause this, but I feel responsible anyway. My magic is supposed to help. I know that it is. But it isn't enough."

"You are not responsible for solving an issue that has been happening for over 100 years. Your magic is a gift, but it is not the answer to everything. That is too much pressure to put onto one person."

"But the mothers who became pregnant as a result of my magic *are* my responsibility. What happens when they go into labor? What happens when *I* go into labor? The risks are even greater." Panic is laced in her words. I do my best to keep mine steady.

"We will find a solution. I am not going to let anything happen to you or our babies. We will monitor closely. We will track any patterns that might be the cause for heavy bleeding. We will remain hopeful that because your magic promotes healthy breeding, that the conditions remain healthy throughout the entire pregnancy and birth. We have not had anyone deliver who has been exposed to your magic."

"I just love them so much already."

I lower my hands to her rounded stomach. "I do too. Their heartbeats are strong. I check them every morning when I wake up and every night after you fall asleep," I confess. "We have three healthy babies, and we are going to do everything that we can to keep it that way. Okay?"

Rowan nods.

"And that means not overusing your power. Now that we know that your magic cannot heal, please promise me that you will not try again. Help support Heka but not with your magic. We do not know what side effects it could cause."

"I know. I'm sorry. I honestly didn't mean to use so much. It was just so heartbreaking."

I lift her chin to place a gentle kiss on her lips. Then, I pick her up and carry her to bed. Rowan falls asleep in my arms, exhausted from the taxing day. I lay awake for hours, feeling the smallest kicks as I hold her stomach.

The next morning, Bade barges into our room, causing both Rowan and myself to suddenly wake.

"Shit, sorry," Bade says as he looks up at the ceiling.

Rowan pulls a blanket around her body while I climb out of bed to find her a shirt. "Is there a reason for this early wakeup call?" I ask Bade.

"I just received word from one of my outposts that Dreena has made camp in my lands. She has a group of about 40 supporters."

Rowan gasps. "She has 40 with her? How many more does she have throughout the territories?"

"We do not know. But there are bands on the move in both Nightfang and Nighthowl. We have been tracking their movements."

"To Nightfury?"

"It looks like it. Based on intel, we predicted that she would try to make camp there. It is the only territory remote enough to go undetected. Unfortunately for her, we knew she was coming and were able to find her right away. I am going to go and shut this down myself. My Beta will remain here a few days longer to keep security going while I am gone but reach out if you need anything else. I will be assembling a team once I have my eyes on the situation."

Bade turns to leave but Rowan stops him. "Please be careful."

"Always," he says before he walks out the door.

"Will he be okay?" Rowan asks me.

"Yes. Bade knows how to take care of himself. His outposts are remote, but he will call in plenty of backup and not attack until he has enough support. Even if he is outnumbered, the only wolves that can match him in power are Griff and myself. He also has a powerful advantage when it comes to ambushing a camp."

"What is that?"

"You know how I have extra sensitive hearing?"

"Yeah."

"Bade has advanced vision. He can see much further than others and he can see thermal outputs."

"I'm sorry to say, Big Guy, but I think your brother's party trick is cooler than yours," she giggles.

I chuckle and tickle her side. It is nice to hear her laugh this morning after such a rough day yesterday. "That may be true," I say, "but mine is still cooler than Griff's."

"What can he do?"

"He has an advanced sense of smell."

She wrinkles her nose. "That could be amazing or terrible. I don't think that there is an in between."

"Maybe after you have our babies, we should hide their soiled linens around his quarters to see how long it takes him to find them."

Rowan doubles over laughing. "That would be such a cruel prank. Let's do it!"

"But for now, let's go back to bed. You know I cannot start my day without having a taste of your sweet pussy." Rowan's eyes blaze with heat as I rip my shirt off of her and dive between her thighs. I make her come twice before she begs for me to fill her ass. It really is the best way to start a day.

Chapter Twenty

I am officially three months pregnant, though I think that I look closer to six. My belly has fully popped and word has spread through the village that I am expecting triplets. I spend most of my days with Heka going on house calls and learning how to be a midwife.

Maha was in yesterday for an appointment and War was able to confirm that she is pregnant with twins. They are so incredibly happy to be expecting, and I am hopeful that I will be able to help others in the future.

As a whole, we have seen a boost in pregnancies since my arrival—we are up to around 50 expectant mothers, including Maha. Heka believes that just being around me increases the chances for people to conceive, even without my intentionally helping. Without knowing the success rate of healthy deliveries, I have decided that I will not intentionally use magic at the moment. I need to know that I am not causing losses. All of the plants that I have grown are thriving, but I cannot handle the stress of taking further risks with people.

Between the late nights assisting births and attending appointments during the day, I find small chunks of time where I can retreat to Helen's hideaway. I feel so relaxed in this room. I can't help but feel closer to War's mother when I am here. I know that she would have appreciated me bringing it back to life. The plants and furniture make the space feel cozy while the skylights let in the perfect amount of afternoon sun.

War has been busy working with hunting parties as well as assisting with the Nightfury pack while Bade is away. He has been gone for some time now. He sent an update saying that he has eyes on Dreena's camp and that he is waiting for his backup to arrive. He hasn't actually seen Dreena at the camp, but that doesn't mean she isn't there. She knows that she needs to lay low while her supporters are drawing attention with their movements.

"There you are," War startles me from my thoughts. He sits down next to me and pulls me into his side.

"I didn't mean to hide from you. I was just resting."

"Are you feeling okay?"

"Yeah. I feel great, actually. Sleep is starting to get a little uncomfortable though. You know, if I was in my world, I would only now be starting to show. It is crazy to me that in just a couple of months, we will have three babies to take care of."

"Do the midwives still think that you will deliver around 6 months?"

"Yes, but it is really anyone's guess. Griffin has found a few texts discussing births between different shifter species, like wolf and panther or wolf and bear, but their gestation periods are similar to wolves, so it is hard to tell. From what was recorded, babies born in those pairings took after one parent in terms of shifting, not a mix of both. So, it would be reasonable to assume that our babies might not have the ability to shift."

"They will be perfect either way."

I give him a smile. I worry that our children will feel different if they cannot shift like their peers, but I know that they will be loved fiercely no matter what abilities they have.

"Do you remember much about your mother?" I ask.

War is quiet for a while before he speaks. "I remember how kind and patient she was," he says. "My
241

brothers and I were not an easy lot to wrangle but she enjoyed the chaos of it all. Her wolf was very protective of us."

"I wish I could have met her. I have had that thought before but even more so now that I know I am pregnant with triplets."

"I believe she kept journals while she was alive. I cannot believe I did not think of it before. I will have Griff find them for you. Maybe they will provide some answers."

"I would love that. I want to honor her in some way."

"She would have loved you, Sunshine. I know that your parents did not show you the love that you deserved, but she would have."

War wipes the tears from my cheeks and then pulls me into an unhurried kiss. This kiss is not meant to heat things up between us—though I do feel a pulse in my core. It is a promise of his love for me. War gives me his love and support unconditionally, every day. While our love is grand, it is the little moments where I become overwhelmed by it.

I feel it when he feeds me before taking anything for himself.

I feel it when he tracks me down in the middle of the day, even though he has other things that he probably should be doing, just to make sure that I am doing okay.

I feel it when he shaves my legs because he knows that I feel more comfortable—even though I am probably the only person in this entire world who feels that way.

I feel his love when he shares bits of himself that I know he usually keeps hidden. And I give all of my love back to him freely. Our love is intense and wild, but it is more than I ever thought I would find—more than I ever thought I deserved. I am just a barista with more issues than I have money in the bank, but for some reason, I am loved by this incredible man.

These pregnancy hormones are definitely getting to me, because I now have tears streaming down my face. War looks at me, wondering what has made me upset.

"These are happy tears. Apparently, I cry all of the time now." War chuckles and gives me another kiss.

"I love you, Ro."

"I love you too, Big Guy. So much."

"I should get back to work," War says begrudgingly. "I have reports of the hunting patterns being disturbed and I need to figure out why."

"Do you think it is because of the weather?" It has been even warmer than normal these last few days. It feels like August in New York instead of the spring temperatures that we should be experiencing.

"I think that it might be related to the trouble that Dreena is stirring up. Travel is always permitted throughout the territories, but most of the time, it is small groups visiting family or hunting parties who follow planned routes. We all know to respect the land and to not take too much, but any groups moving through are bound to scare prey away."

"What can we do about it?"

"First, we need to figure out what the cause is. Then, we will just have to shift our routes to make up for the change. There is still plenty to eat, but we might shift to having less meat for our meals during these warmer months, especially in the more densely populated areas."

"I can help grow more fruits and vegetables, if that would help."

"Thank you, love. I will let you know if we need to. The Mother has always provided plenty. We just need to listen."

"We have six mothers due any day now. I told Heka that I can help with deliveries since multiple could happen at the same time."

"Just make sure that you bring someone with you, or let me know where you are headed through the bond. I will worry if I do not know where you are."

"Of course," I promise. "Between Heka, Eden, and Maha, we should be able to team up so that none of us will be alone during a difficult birth."

War left to meet up with Zeke while I remained in the hideaway for a little longer. When my stomach begins to rumble, I make my way down to the kitchen to grab a pre-dinner snack. The fruit in this world is similar to what I am used to, but the taste is more intense. It is really delicious. I am in the middle of sneaking a bite of cobbler when Griffin walks in.

I must look like a deer in headlights because he chuckles at me.

"Your secret is safe with me," he says. He walks over to the ice box and pulls out some kind of sweet cream, scooping out a dollop and putting it on my plate. "It is even better with this."

A moan escapes me as I take a bite. My cheeks instantly heat as he throws his head back and laughs.

"That good, huh?"

"It really is," I reply.

"War said that you are interested in reading our mother's journals? There are many of them, but I pulled a few that were from when she was pregnant with us." He sets the journals down on the counter.

"Thank you so much!" I open one of them up, glancing at a random page. "Her handwriting is beautiful."

Griffin nods his head in agreement. "These are some of my favorite books. You probably cannot detect it, but I can smell her jasmine scent on the pages."

"I promise I will take good care of them."

"I know you will. I'm sorry that I did not think to share them before. I was so focused on finding information on everything else that I forgot we have this record to pull from."

I read through more of the entry, smiling at the mention of feeling the babies move throughout the night. Wait, I can't believe I didn't realize this before when I was working with Griffin in the library, but how can I understand this at all? I doubt it was written in my language. So, I ask him.

"Ah, I was wondering when you might figure that out," he chuckles. "I suspect that one of the powers that transferred over to you from War was the ability to understand languages. You are still speaking in your native language, but you have not noticed when we slip random words from our language while speaking to you. Bade, War, and I had a bet on if you would notice or not."

"Seriously?" I can't help but laugh. "How long has this been going on?"

"Since the first time I saw you reading without difficulty."

"And you weren't going to tell me?"

"To be fair, if I told you I would have lost the bet. War thought that you would figure it out within the first month of you being here. Bade did not think you ever would. I bet that it would be more than three but less than six months. So, I won."

I laugh again. "Well, what did you win?"

"Bragging rights, obviously. And I get to reinstate game night. It is something that we did when we were younger, but our father put a stop to it because we are so competitive."

"And you think now is a good time to start it back up? I don't imagine you are any less competitive."

"Ah, but now we have you to keep War in check. He was always the worst loser."

I love the relationship that War has with his brothers. I feel tears start to well up in my eyes and try to blink them back before they fall. I'm not quick enough though and Griffin notices.

"Hey, please don't cry." He wraps his arm around my shoulder. "I did not mean to make you upset. I promise that the bet was all in good fun. We did not mean anything by it."

I wipe away the tears and smile. "It isn't that. I just miss my sisters. We aren't triplets like you, but we were incredibly close. I am happy that War has that with you."

"We will find them if they are here," he promises. "And if they are still back in your world, please know that you have us too now. I know that Bade is a grump but surely War and I make up for everything that he lacks."

I chuckle at his joke. "You know, if I had to be transported to a different world, I am glad that I ended up here."

"Will you tell me about your sisters?"

Griffin and I sit at the kitchen counter talking about Ramsey and Reese for hours. I mostly tell him about recent years, the time after Ramsey gained custody of us and we lived together in our tiny New York apartment. He listens as I laugh and cry and eat the entire pan of cobbler. He shares some stories about growing up with War and Bade. He has a lot more memories than I do—but that will happen when you have already lived for 100 years.

Late in the evening, Lycus and War join us in the kitchen. Lycus looks for the cobbler and is confused as to where it went. Griffin and I laugh so hard that I almost pee my pants.

I do miss my sisters, but I am so happy to be a part of this family too. I go to bed that night with a full stomach and an even fuller heart.

Chapter Twenty-One

"You are doing great!" I encourage the mother. This is the third delivery that Eden and I have been called out to this week. Heka and Maha assisted another mother late last night and had just arrived back at the lodge when we were notified of this labor. We have paired up so that we can get some rest. With six expectant mothers due this week, we have been stretched thin. So far, we have only had one loss. It was a twin pregnancy and one of the babies did not make it. But, the other did and the mother did not suffer from major blood loss. The other deliveries have been for single babies and other than one mother losing quite a lot of blood, everything went well.

The baby that is being born right now appears to be caught in the birthing canal. I hold the mother's hand while Eden tries to reposition the baby. If this happened back in New York, this mother would need a c-section. That is not an option here. It is far too risky.

Eden wipes the sweat off of her brow once she is able to work the baby's shoulder free. "Go ahead and push," Eden says.

The mother gives one final push and Eden catches the baby as she makes her way into this world. The baby makes a loud cry, and we all take a relieved breath.

"She is beautiful," I say as the mother holds her daughter to her chest.

Walking back into the lodge a few hours later, I am exhausted and in need of a bath. Eden's home was nearby so she went straight home after we got the mother and baby settled. I stop by Heka's small clinic in the lodge to record the birth and then head towards my room. I really need to sleep. I quickly get bathed before crawling into bed to sleep. War is gone today charting new hunting routes with Zeke and Arlo and I plan to sleep until he gets back.

I am woken to knocking on my bedroom door. "Rowan? It's Eden. We have another house call."

I sit up and rub my eyes. It is still light outside, so I must have only been asleep for a couple of hours. I climb out of bed and quickly dress before opening my door. Eden stands in the hall, looking as worn out as I feel.

"I didn't think that we had anyone else due this week." I grab one of our Maternity bags that we keep prepared by the door.

"This female is not due, but we were called out due to bleeding," she explains quickly.

I nod and walk with her out the door. Eden is quiet on our walk through Nightfang. We are both running on fumes, but our house calls should quiet down for a little while after this.

"Who are we seeing?" I ask.

"I do not think that you have met her yet," Eden replies. I nod my head and walk a little faster to keep up with Eden. There is still much of the pack that I don't know. Because Nightfang is mostly hunters and their families, the pack members are always coming and going between the village and the outposts.

We wind deeper and deeper into the village, coming to a stop right outside a house. The houses in the village are all similar in their design. Most have an open living, dining, and kitchen area which leads to two bedrooms and a bathroom. Some of the houses have more bedrooms added on to accommodate any pups that they have been blessed with, like Eden's home. Eden steps up to the front door and opens it after giving one knock. "Midwives," she says as we enter.

Most of the house is dark, with not much in the terms of furniture or decorations. My guess is that this family has recently returned after being away. Like Eden, it is possible that the family typically travels with hunting parties but has returned due to the pregnancy.

I follow Eden into the back of the house where the bedrooms are. Stepping into the room, I immediately know that something is wrong. Eden pushes me further into the room, making me trip over my own feet, and then blocks my path to the door.

Across the room, Zuri stands with a sneer on her face.

My hackles instantly raise. "What is going on?" I look back to Eden for some kind of explanation. Her eyes are filled with tears.

"I am so sorry, Rowan," she says. "She took my children. She told me that if I brought you here so that she could talk to you, she would give them back. It's my pups, Ro."

Looking at Zuri, it is clear that she does not want to have a friendly conversation with me. If she did, she could have come to the lodge herself. No. I am in danger. *My* babies are in danger. I wild growl rips itself from my throat. The betrayal that I feel from Eden's actions cut deep. She is my friend. I trusted her. If she would have told me what had happened, War would have helped her find them. Griffin would have helped—he is at one of his outposts right now but would have rushed home to follow their scent. We all would have helped. Turning my back on Eden, I face Zuri straight on. She looks over my shoulder, rattling off what I assume is an address, before the door behind me snicks closed. She fucking left me here. Locked in a room with a pissed off wolf shifter.

Keeping my face neutral, I reach out to War through our bond. He already knew that I was heading out for a delivery, hopefully he is close. The glint of a knife catches my attention as I struggle to keep myself calm.

"Zuri is here. She has a knife, War. It was a trap."

I can hear War roar through the bond. *"Help will be there soon. Do you know where you are?"*

Zuri walks towards me as I back away from her. I keep going until I am back against the wall. There is nowhere for me to go.

"We went four streets past Eden's house off of the main road. Please hurry. She is going to hurt me. I...I'm scared.."

"What are you doing here, Zuri?"

"Oh, I just thought that we should have a little chat, catch up on all the ways you have ruined my life." Ruined her life? The last report that we received about Zuri, she had worked hard to replace all of the items that were stolen or destroyed. Her guard left once everything was replaced.

"Keep calm and try to get her talking. Stall," War says.

Taking a deep breath, I try to think of a route out of this mess. This is not the first time a bully has had me backed into a corner—but Ramsey is not here to stand up for me. I am on my own until War can get here. What would Ramsey do?

"What do you mean? I thought that we ended things on a good note. I heard that you fulfilled your duties..."

"My duties? You mean working day and night so that you and your *Mate,*" she spits out the word, "can live in luxury while the rest of us are struggling to just survive?"

But that's not true. I shake my head. The pack is doing more than surviving. When everyone works together, all three packs thrive. I have seen with my own eyes how the community comes together to make sure that everyone has more than what they need.

"Where is Sylas, Zuri? Zya?"

Her eyes are wild, unfocused. She continues to stalk close to me, taunting me as she flips the knife in the air and catches it. "Sylas? You don't know? I assumed you would have heard by now. It was your spell, after all, that ruined my life."

"What spell, Zuri? I don't know any spells."

Zuri cackles. "That is what you want everyone to believe, isn't it? But I know the truth."

"What truth? I don't know what you are talking about."

"You took my hands, pretending to show kindness but instead, you cursed me. You are a witch—just like Dreena warned. A witch in disguise."

I keep my voice calm, trying not to show her how scared I am. "I did not curse you, Zuri. I do not have any magic that could do that."

Sneering, Zuri lunges closer. "Of course you will not admit it. But I know! I know that you cursed me. Your little witchy friend showed up days ago to help punish me. She showed up and he chose her. He chose me for years but then she showed up and he chose her. She is not even a wolf! She is just a kid. He chose her and she cannot even bond with him for years."

I am having trouble following what Zuri is saying. I keep my focus on the knife she is waving around. I know that I cannot fight against a wolf, so I need to keep her in her human form. I need to get the knife away from her.

"Who did Sylas choose?"

"Pay attention!" she yells. "He chose the child! The other witch brought her, and he chose her over me."

The other witch?

"You met another human? What did she look like?"

"I met another *witch*," she spits at me. "She brought the child to Sylas and he chose her. She is not even a wolf. She reeked of bear!"

A bear child? I know that there are other shifters in this world. If I remember correctly, the bear territory shares a border with Nightfury.

Desperate for more information, I ask again. "What did the human look like? What color was her hair?"

"Why does that matter? You are missing the point. He was told that the child has a piece of his soul and he didn't question it. He threw me away like trash. Like the years that we spent together meant nothing." Her voice cracks as unshed tears glisten in the low light. "Sylas chose me for years before your kind showed up and cursed me."

"What color was the human's hair?" I ask again.

"Copper," she snarls. "She was tiny and weak like you. Sickly. But, that doesn't matter anymore. She will be gone soon enough."

Copper. Reese. Reese is in this world and she brought a bear child to Sylas? "Sylas found his True Mate?"

"True Mate?" She growls. "The witch used her magic to trick him—just like you did with the Alpha. But you will not get away with it. Get rid of the witch, get rid of the curse. Soon, all of the witches will be dealt with. Dreena will see to it. The copper one is probably already gone. She was so sickly. But don't worry. You will see her soon in whatever afterlife you sink down into."

Reese is sick? What did she do to her? I need to get out of here. I need to find her.

"Where is the other human?"

Zuri lets out a deranged laugh. I can feel her spit land on my face as she speaks. "I gave her to Dreena's pack. They will have their fun and then destroy her. One by one, we will rid the world of your kind. You leech the power from our world and destroy our way of life."

Zuri keeps rambling but I can no longer focus on her words. I look around the room, trying to find a way out. I take a small step, but she lunges again, pushing me back. She has me pinned against the wall as she waves her knife around.

I can't help but shudder as she presses her hand to my stomach. "It is a shame that your babies will die too—but the Alpha should have known better than to Mate with an outsider. Maybe next time he will choose a stronger partner."

I bare my teeth as she pats my stomach.

"Don't like that, do you? He will move on, you know? You might have tricked him with your magic but once you are dead, he will find someone else. Maybe he will even choose me," she taunts. "Oh, how poetic that would be."

Quicker than I expected, she moves. Her right hand holds the knife as she raises it above her head and stabs down. I can hear the sound of the blade cutting through the air before it reaches my skin. I don't have space to move out of its path, so I twist and turn, the blade piercing my lower back instead of my heart. She pulls the knife out of my wound, and I can feel the gush of blood as it runs down my hip and onto the floor. I was trying to protect my babies, but they are in danger anyway.

Air is knocked out of my lungs as I crumple to the floor. Zuri's body is yanked away from mine, her blood mixing with mine as I lay curled up on my side. I hold a protective hand over my unborn babies, praying to The Mother, The Moon, and all other deities that I did enough to save them.

Blinking the blood from my eyes, I once again come face to face with a beautiful black wolf. But this is not my wolf. My wolf has ice blue eyes and this wolf's eyes are green. My sisters and I all have green eyes, but these are deeper, saturated in a way that can only happen in this world. This must be a dream. A gentle way for my brain to ease me into the nothingness of death.

Death's eyes look upon me with understanding, love, and so much fear it is hard to fully comprehend in my deteriorating state.

"I love you, War. Always. Please save our babies. I'm sorry I couldn't."

The world around me goes black.

Chapter Twenty-Two

I storm through the door to find my father cradling Rowan in his arms. Heka is trying to tend to her wound, and they are both shaking, visibly upset.

I gently take her from his arms and hold her close to my body, sinking down onto the floor in the entryway. I lay her down onto her side so that I can look at her wound without putting any pressure on her belly. Shifting back into my wolf, I lap at her back, trying to heal her.

Heka and my father try to approach, but I growl at them and shift my body over Rowan's. I listen closely. Rowan is breathing and her heartbeat is still strong, but she is pale and not healing herself. I listen to the babies. One of the heartbeats is slower than the others.

"One of the babies is hurt," I growl at my father and Heka. They both nod their understanding but keep their distance. She should be healing herself, but because one of the babies is in trouble, her body is focusing on healing the baby instead.

I can hear Heka and my father talking quietly, trying to figure out what can be done, while I try to heal her in the only way I know how.

Suddenly, the front door bangs open and a stranger rushes towards us. I growl and snap my teeth at the woman. She is shaking, sobbing as she looks past me at Ro. but takes a single step back when she realizes that I will not let her get closer.

"Please let me help," she pleads, her voice quiet but firm. "I need to see her. Maybe I can help. I would never hurt her. I would die to save her. Please let me help."

Unable to trust anyone right now, I continue growling. The woman takes another cautious step closer, and I lunge, knocking her down and away from my Mate.

Out of nowhere, Griff's wolf flies into the room, jumps over top of the stranger, and forces me away with his shoulder. He then positions himself between the woman and me.

"She is mine," he growls. *"You will not hurt my Mate!"*

What the fuck? His Mate? I shake my head, trying to focus through the aggression that I feel.

"Please let me see her," the woman says, drawing my attention back to her as she scrambles to sit back up. "I am a nurse; I might be able to help. Please let me help Rowan."

A nurse? She knows Rowan?

I shift so that I can communicate with her better. Griff shifts too but keeps himself positioned between the nurse and me.

"Ramsey?" I ask.

The woman jerks her head in a frantic nod. "Yes! Please let me help Ro. I just found her again. I cannot lose her! I will do everything that I can to help her."

I step aside, hoping that this is not a trick. Griff gives me a look, encouraging me to trust her. She looks like she could be Rowan's sister. She has similar features, though her hair is a dark brown and she stands a little taller.

Ramsey hesitantly steps around Griff, giving him a strange look before kneeling next to Rowan. She has tears flooding her face and she slowly moves her shaking hands to examine the wound.

"She is pregnant?" she asks. I pick Rowan back up, cradling her in my arms as I sit on the floor. If I am going to let someone this close, I need to be holding her.

Ramsey is focused as she assesses Rowan.

"Are you bonded?" she asks.

"Yes. She should be healing herself but one of the babies is in distress. Her body is not able to keep up with healing them both."

"She is losing too much blood," she says, pressing firmly on the knife wound. "Please be okay. You need to fight this, Rowan. Do you hear me? You need to fight." Turning back to me she asks, "Do you know how long the blade was?"

My father steps closer. "It was about the size of my hand," he tells her.

Ramsey continues talking to Rowan softly, begging her to get better, while she holds pressure onto the wound.

That is when it happens. Ramsey's hands begin to glow with silver moonlight. Her eyes are shut, and I'm not sure she even realizes it is happening. It is the same kind of power that I witnessed when Rowan covered my mother's statue in flowering vines. But no plants spring to life. I look over to Griff. His eyes are wide but he gives me a subtle nod, not wanting to draw too much attention.

I look back down to where Ramsey is holding Rowan and watch as the hole in her back begins to stitch itself closed. We all hold our breath as Ramsey uses magic to heal her sister.

Rowan gasps and sits up, looking around as if she just woke up from a dream. "Ramsey?" she questions softly.

"Rowan!" Ramsey leans forward and pulls Rowan into a tight hug. "I am so happy that you are okay! I thought that I lost you right when I found you again."

Both sisters are crying as they hug each other.

"I have a lot to fill you in on, but first, what happened?" Ro looks to me for answers, but I am unsure how to put it all into words.

"How much do you remember?" I ask her, placing a kiss on her forehead.

She pauses to think but then starts talking. "Zuri attacked me. Eden brought me to her." I growl. "Zuri had her kids. She believed it was the only way to get them back. Zuri was talking about witches and how we ruined her life." Rowan gasps. "I think she met Reese! She said that she met a witch with copper hair. That has to be Reese, right? And then she stabbed me. I tried to protect our babies but she was too fast. And then I saw a wolf. I thought that it was you," she turns to me, "but he didn't have your eyes." She pauses and then looks at my father. "It was you, wasn't it?" He gives her a nod and a small smile. "Thank you for helping me."

"Thank goodness for your accelerated healing," Ramsey adds. "Estelle told me that bonded wolves share traits, but I didn't know if that would work for humans too."

"You healed her, Angel," Griff says as he takes a step towards Ramsey.

"What? How did I heal her? I just put pressure on the wound to slow the bleeding. That wouldn't be enough to heal a stab wound."

"Look at your hands," he says, nodding to where her hands lay gently at her sides.

We all look down at Ramsey's hands, which are now covered in moon markings.

"Moon Touched," Rowan says with awe. Ramsey looks at the markings on her hands and then to the markings on our chests.

"It appears it is me as well," Griff says, holding his hands out to show matching tattoos to the ones marking Ramsey.

Rowan gulps. "Does that mean that you are..."

"Mates." Griff confirms. Ramsey looks at him, her eyes going wide, and then she collapses to the ground.

Chapter Twenty-Three

"Did you get Ramsey settled okay," War asks me as I enter our bedroom.

It has been several hours since I was magically healed after Zuri's attack. Heka was able to wake Ramsey up with smelling salts after she passed out. We do not know if it was from the stress of the incident, using magic for the first time, or the shock of having a Mate, but she seems to be okay.

"Yes. She is refusing to sleep in Griffin's quarters though."

"His wolf is not going to tolerate being separated from her now that they have found each other. I tried sleeping elsewhere when I first found you, but I could not handle it. I ended up sleeping on the floor beside the bed during your recovery."

"I know. And she is flat out refusing to discuss the whole Mate thing. That is why I set her up in the room connected to the library," I say with a grin.

War wraps me in his arms and I tuck my face against his bare chest. "Clever girl."

"She will come around. I think that this is all just a lot for her to process all at one time. Ramsey is very pragmatic. Once she understands the situation more fully, she will accept it."

"The next full moon is three weeks away," he reminds me.

"They don't have to bond at the first full moon though, right?"

"Technically, no. But with the threat of Dreena still out there, Griff's wolf is going to push for it to keep her safe."

"I will talk to her." Hopefully after a couple of days of rest, she will be in the right mindset to listen. "Have you heard back from Bade?"

War had sent an update to Bade, but he did not reply right away. War thinks that he is probably in the thick of his mission right now and is blocking out all distractions.

"Not yet. But he heard me even if he did not respond. If Dreena's pack has Reese, they are going to bring her to their camp in Nightfury. Bade will find her."

"I am just so worried about her. Zuri said that she is sick."

"I know, love. We will get it all figured out."

War and I slide into bed, ready to put an end to this crazy day. He tucks me up against the pillows and then sinks down to rest his head on my belly.

"You scared me today. I thought I would lose you—or the babies," he confesses quietly.

"I know," I reply, running my fingers through his hair. "I was scared too. But we are okay. Whatever magic Ramsey used made me feel even better than I did before. Even my normal pregnancy aches are gone. How is it possible that she gained her moon magic before bonding? We didn't receive our markings until after our bond."

"I am not sure, Sunshine. Something must have triggered it. Griff is going to look into it some more. He is still looking for that passage from The Mother that he remembers seeing years ago."

"Ramsey could probably help him get through books faster, if she could understand the language. She would need to bond with him first though. Speaking of which—I hear we will be starting up a family game night again in the near future." I poke him in his side, causing him to chuckle.

"I would have told you if I could, but a bet is a bet. I was not allowed to interfere. Besides, I thought you would figure it out much sooner. I have been calling you Sunshine in our language for months."

"Seriously? I really can't even tell the difference. You could be speaking to me in a completely different language and it all sounds like English to me. This is so weird."

Not wanting to bring up a sore topic—but needing to—I ask about Eden.

War growls. "Arlo confirmed that their children were scared but unharmed. I think that it would be best if they return to an outpost after their twins are born."

"We cannot force them to move."

"I can order them to go wherever the fuck I want," he grumbles. "They can be banished. I will not do it, but Eden could be killed for her betrayal. Moving them to an outpost is the kindest punishment I can offer."

"But Arlo is your best hunter."

"And he will continue to hunt. But I cannot allow Eden to remain here after their babies are born. I will never be able to trust her again."

"I understand. I really do. But she was just trying to protect her children. The pain that she caused my heart was almost greater than the one I received in my back—but I cannot blame her for what she did for her children. I would do anything to save ours."

"You would never have put her in danger like she did with you."

"Maybe not. But I can still understand why she did it."

"I could have lost you. It is unforgivable."

War listens to my belly for a while longer, whispering encouraging words to our babies, telling them to grow big and strong.

"Three strong heartbeats," he says quietly.

Chapter Twenty-Four

(About Seven Months Later)

"It is time to make your birthday wish, Sunshine." War's body presses up against my back as we stand in the garden, surrounded by the life that I helped create with my magic.

"I don't know what to wish for," I admit, turning in his arms.

If someone would have told me a year ago that I would be standing here today, I would have thought that they were on drugs. I am no longer the 21-year-old barista and a green thumb hobbyist.

"You know," I say, "when I first woke up here, I thought there was a good chance I was going to end up as a victim on a true crime podcast."

War laughs. "I will happily hunt you down if you feel like running." He takes my mouth in a bruising kiss. "Just say the word and you can be my prey," he adds against my lips.

"And what if I want to be the hunter?" I ask breathlessly, enjoying where this is going.

"Then I will gladly run. But I would not make it far before I surrender and let you do anything that you want with me."

"I'm sure you would," I smirk. Looking around to see that we truly are alone, I slowly take off my clothes, piece by piece. War's eyes darken with hunger as he watches me. Once I am completely bare, I lift up onto my tip toes to place an innocent kiss on my Mate's lips. "Be a good boy and give me a five-minute head start," I tell him as I take off running towards the trees that surround our home.

A year ago, I woke up from a nightmare and found myself in this new world with no idea that I would end up in the arms of my soulmate.

Keep running. War will give me a fair head start, but once he starts running, he will not take it easy on me.

His wolf's instincts will kick in and he will catch me. The thought of being caught causes an ache in my center. We have played this scene out a few times before and it is even better each time.

The air becomes thick with anticipation. A flash of lightning strikes the sky in the distance. I shiver at the thought of being caught out in the rain, naked, with nowhere to go.

Tripping over a raised root, I fall to the ground, collapsing onto the forest floor. Catching my breath, I lay still and look up at the moon as I wait for my Mate to find me.

Turning my head at the sound of a branch snapping, I once again come face to face with a wolf. He is huge—at least double the size of a wolf from the world I came from. His all-black coat and ice blue eyes pierce straight to my soul, just like the first time I saw him.

I reach out as the wolf stalks closer. My body is on fire, not knowing what he is going to do to me first. I snake my hand down my body, moaning as I relieve some of the pressure with my fingers. I hear a low growl right before he leaps, shifting into his human form, and tackling me so that his body covers my own.

"You are a naughty little prize, giving yourself pleasure when that is my job," he whispers in my ear.

"What are you going to do about it?" I ask.

"I am going to take what is mine." He growls, spearing his cock into my wet pussy. I scream as my body struggles to accommodate his size. Rain starts to pour down on us as he fucks me hard into the dirt path beneath me. I can feel my back getting scratched up from the rocks and sticks that lay beneath me. I sink my nails into War's back, marking him the same way that I am being marked.

He fucks me through my first orgasm, not stopping even as my clit becomes painfully overstimulated. I cry out, spasming around his cock as he growls into my neck, spilling himself deep within me.

Flipping me onto my hands and knees, he presses his cum covered cock into my ass, reaching forward to hold my neck with his large hand. Tears fill my eyes as he thrusts hard and deep into my tight hole, limiting my air supply as he takes me from behind over and over.

"You are so fucking beautiful taking everything that I give you." Thunder and lightning fill the air as our bodies crash together over and over again. It is too much—and I cannot get enough.

"More," I whisper, not having the ability to speak louder with his hand on my throat.

Taking his free hand, War spanks my dripping pussy. Hard. The pain sends me over the edge as I barrel into oblivion. The world around me goes dark.

"Fuck, Sunshine. Are you okay?" His words are full of worry as he pulls me back into consciousness. All I can do in return is smile. I no longer have a form, unable to lift my limbs, it feels as if I am made of jello. My body has been completely drained of energy—and I have been remade on the forest floor with the force of my orgasm.

Vaguely aware of my surroundings, I realize War has carried me through the storm back to our home. I am still floating as he washes the mud from our bodies and heals the scratches on my back. Tucking me into our bed, he pulls me close, holding me flush to his skin as I regain control over myself.

"Forever," I say, my throat raspy from screaming in pleasure.

"What?" he asks, his face relieved that I am able to speak again.

"Forever. That is my birthday wish. I want this forever."

"Orgasmic bliss?" He chuckles.

I snort. "That too, Big Guy. But I mean this life. I want to help the pack with my magic. I want to raise our babies in this amazing community, where they will feel loved every day. I want to give you my mornings and my nights. And I want to take the same from you. All of it."

"Forever." He smiles, placing a gentle kiss on my forehead.

I nod and return his smile as I let my eyelids close, drifting off to sleep in the arms of my Mate. Forever.

Author's Note

Thank you so much for reading my debut novel. Becoming an author is a dream that I have had since I was a little girl living between the pages of fairy tales. It means the world to me that you picked up my book and gave my words a chance.

Rowan and her sisters have been characters floating around in my head for a long time. It feels amazing to finally breathe life into them. Before the story fully formed in my head, I knew that Rowan was the sister who needed to arrive first. She is spontaneous, a little impatient, and has a sense of humor that lends well to being magically transported to another world where her super-hot soulmate has a habit of shifting into a giant wolf.

While Rowan and War do receive their happily ever after in *Nightfang*, you do not need to say goodbye yet. Both characters will be making frequent appearances as the story continues in Ramsey and Griffin's book, *Nighthowl*.

Keep reading for a sneak peek at *Nighthowl*.

Content Warning

This book contains strong language, sexually explicit scenes, discussions of sexual assault, drugging, violence, self-harm, panic attacks, kidnapping, trafficking, child neglect, societal infertility, pregnancy, childbirth, and loss.

Ramsey is a survivor. While her experiences are discussed and shown via nightmares, the assault happened prior to her arriving in this world and is not at the hands of our MMC. Griffin is a supportive partner who loves Ramsey through her healing.

The Moon Touched Chronicles

Nightfang

Nighthowl

Nightfury

The Sun Kissed Scrolls

Lightclaw

(Coming Soon)

<u>www.rubyellisauthor.com</u>

Chapter One

Everything around me is dirty.

My clothes? Dirty.

The floor? Dirty.

My skin? Dirty.

Their hands on me? Dirty.

Hunger gnaws at my stomach as I struggle to keep my eyes open. It used to be a familiar feeling starvation— but it has been years since I last endured the pain. My eyes drift closed and I am taken back to those days early in my life. Days and nights when I rationed the food that I took from school so that my sisters could eat. When their whimpers and cries were the ones that I heard at night instead of the noises that surround me now.

I sit up, shaken back to the very real Hell that I am living in now, and try to breathe.

The air that I pull into my lungs is thick with cigarette smoke and the smell of unwashed bodies. I am alone in my cell. Empty. Just the shell of the person I once was as company. There were others, but they are gone now. I don't know where they went but I could hear their cries as they were taken. My sisters cried when they were taken from me too—but I got them back.

The women from the cell won't be coming back.

Only men.

The men visit me in my cell. Sometimes they take me to another room. But I always return to my cell after.

I don't know why they keep me. I wish they wouldn't. I can find my sisters in another life. This one isn't worth living anymore.

No.

If I allow myself to think like that, I will never make it out of here alive. I need to focus. I need water. I need to get clean.

I need to wash this place from my soul.

The walls are closing in around me. It is suffocating. I need to breathe but I cannot get air.

Footsteps.

No. No no no! I make myself small. I hide in the corner. Please keep walking. Please choose someone else.

The footsteps stop outside my cell. No! Please no! I am still dirty!

"Wake up, Angel." The voice is soft and calm. It pulls me from my nightmare.

I look around, unsure as to where I am. The room slowly comes into focus, but the decorated walls are unfamiliar.

I can feel tears running down my face and my throat is burning from screaming in my cell without water.

"You are safe," the voice says. I turn towards the sound and startle when I see a man kneeling by my bed. A bed. I'm not in the cell. I am not in that Hell where monsters feed off of my body as they eat away at my soul.

Not a man. Griffin.

It was just a dream. I let out a relieved breath.

"What are you doing in here?" I ask as I quickly smooth my hair out of my face. I didn't mean for my tone to sound so harsh, but I don't like that he saw me like this. Terrified. Shaking. Weak.

Griffin stays kneeling but backs away from me. His blue eyes turned navy in the darkness of night. "I was in the library," he explains, nodding to the wall behind the headboard of my bed. "You were yelling in your sleep. I apologize for startling you." I cannot read the look that flashes in his eyes before he forces them back into a quiet calm. Was it pity? Fear?

"Oh." Embarrassment makes my cheeks heat. "Well, thank you for waking me. It was just a bad dream." I pull my knees up to my chest and hide my face from his view. He reaches out to touch me but pulls his hand back away before he makes contact.

"Do you want to talk about it?" His voice is like a balm to my frayed edges. I don't know why he has this effect on me. I don't feel safe around any man. Not anymore. But Griffin brings me comfort. It doesn't make any sense. I don't even know him but I have to stop myself from reaching out and running my hands through his hair. He keeps it cut shorter than most males that I have seen in this world. Every time that I have seen him his hair is slightly mussed, like he often runs his hands through it while he is thinking or reading. I desperately want to know if it is as soft as it looks.

Realizing that he asked me a question, I shake my head. I don't want to ever talk about it. I have been having the same nightmares since I arrived in this world. Estelle, Griffin's aunt, tried to get me to open up about it once, but I couldn't. If they knew...No. They cannot know. They would look at me differently. They would see me how I see myself. Broken. Stained.

Logically, I understand that what happened to me was not my fault. I should be able to talk about it. I probably need to talk about it. But I can't. Not yet. Maybe not ever.

"Is there anything that I can get you?" He hands me a cup of water, anticipating my needs before I can voice them. My hands are shaking so bad that I almost spill the water as I lift it to my mouth. But he does not comment on it. He simply reaches out to steady the cup with his own grip.

I shake my head again. "It was just a bad dream. I'm okay now." I know that he can hear the lie for what it is, but he gets up and heads towards the door anyway.

Turning back towards me before he leaves the room, I can tell that he is trying to decide if he should leave or stay. "Are you sure that you are okay?" he asks one more time. Stay, my inner voice pleads, but I nod and try to smile. It doesn't quite work but it is the best that I can offer him right now.

As soon as he leaves, I get out of bed and start the bath. I need to get clean. I scrub my skin until it is almost raw and then get dressed again for bed. Rowan had brought me some of her clothes, but I am wearing one of Griffin's shirts. I know that it is his because it smells like him. It brings me comfort even though it shouldn't. He smells like home in a way that I have never been able to find before.

I should wrap my hair in a towel or braid it out of my face, but I am too exhausted, so I let my long strands soak through the shoulders of my borrowed shirt. He was only in here for a few minutes, but I am overwhelmed by the kindness that he showed me—the support that he has shown me from the very start. I'm not sure if I even deserve it. I certainly didn't do anything to warrant it from him. But he offers it anyway.

Inhaling his spicy scent, I pull the blankets up over my head and cry myself back to sleep.